"I didn't mean to upset you," Bates said quietly.

"You did, but it wasn't your fault, it was mine. Everyone talks about Tuckerville as if it's dead. But things *do* happen here. Important things." Rhetta let out a soft sigh. "We got the bank lobby recarpeted. Mary Louise Hopkins taught old Timber how to read after he turned fifty. Lucille Becket lost two teeth in three days. And Jonas Neal donated the use of his land for the church picnic. Now I know those things won't set the world on fire with excitement, but they're important because they're about people—people who care about one another and help each other."

"You're right about Tuckerville," Bates said reflectively. "It is the people that make a town dead or alive. That's why I've come back."

Dear Reader,

Spellbinders! That's what we're striving for. The editors at Silhouette are determined to capture your imagination and win your heart with every single book we publish. Each month, six Special Editions are chosen with *you* in mind.

Our authors are our inspiration. Writers such as Nora Roberts, Tracy Sinclair, Kathleen Eagle, Carole Halston and Linda Howard—to name but a few—are masters at creating endearing characters and heartrending love stories. Their characters are everyday people—just like you and me—whose lives have been touched by love, whose dream and desire suddenly comes true!

So find a cozy, quiet place to read, and create your own special moment with a Silhouette Special Edition.

Sincerely,

Rosalind Noonan
Senior Editor
SILHOUETTE BOOKS

MONIQUE HOLDEN
Tuckerville Revival

Silhouette Special Edition

Published by Silhouette Books New York

America's Publisher of Contemporary Romance

SILHOUETTE BOOKS
300 East 42nd St., New York, N.Y. 10017

ISBN: 0-373-09342-X

First Silhouette Books printing October 1986

America's Publisher of Contemporary Romance

Printed in the U.S.A.

MONIQUE HOLDEN

loves to travel and has even bicycled across Europe, where she acquired a taste for adventure. Her hobbies include tennis, swimming, gardening, needlepoint and redecorating her house. Monique makes her home in Oklahoma, where she lives with her husband, their child and their pet Weimeraner.

NEW MEXICO

OKLAHOMA

ARK.

Amarillo

Dallas

LA.

Abilene

Fort Worth

El Paso

Tuckerville

Pineland

TEXAS

Austin

Jasper

Beaumont

San Antonio

Houston

MEXICO

Corpus Christi

GULF OF MEXICO

TEXAS

Underlined places are fictitious.

Chapter One

"You suppose we'll get any rain?" Nanny Fields looked up at the clouds and then eased back in her white wicker rocker on the front porch of the Tucker Boarding House.

"I heard the weather report about noon and there's a fifty percent chance of rain tonight. I sure hope it pours because then I won't have to water." Rhetta Tucker's cerulean eyes surveyed the fluffy clouds floating slowly across the sky. She dangled her pink leather sandal on the tip of her toes. The sandal dropped from her foot and fell on the porch boards with a hollow clatter. Sliding the other sandal off to join the first, she rubbed the soles of her feet against the glossy light gray floor.

"Yes, ma'am, those geraniums need some water bad." With a hint of disapproval, Nanny Fields eyed the red geraniums nodding from forest-green window boxes in the shade of the porch. Nanny pulled a handkerchief out of her pocket and dabbed at imaginary moisture on her wrinkled neck, which was as dry as a crackling leaf in the fall. She lifted a tea towel full of green beans from the colander that sat between the wicker chairs and placed it in her lap.

Rhetta sighed as the slight afternoon breeze gently lifted the skirt of her strawberry-pink dress, then dropped it. The air was muggy again today, so the late-afternoon breeze felt especially good. She was hot and tired from washing linens for her five boarders and from baking cookies for two hours in the heat of the afternoon.

Lifting her auburn hair off her neck, she stretched languidly. The soft cotton dress pulled up above her knees and fluttered as the breeze caught the skirt again.

Two-year-old Natalie Ford tottered down the side-walk, diaper drooping, teddy bear dragging along behind her through the sandy dirt on the sidewalk. Mrs. Bookerton's shaggy mongrel padded along behind her, bone in mouth, tail plumed, obviously well pleased with himself.

A sleek black sports car zoomed down the street and stopped abruptly at the curb just before the entryway to Rhetta's boarding house. Rhetta and Nanny sat forward a bit, peering with interest at the flashy car.

Black, with lots of chrome. Not many cars drove down this street at all, let alone an expensive-looking car like that. In fact, there wasn't a single sports car in all of Tuckerville.

"Wonder who that could be?" Nanny mused, with the interest all small-town people afford any stranger.

"I don't know. They aren't from around here," Rhetta added. "Nobody in Tuckerville drives a car like that one." Rhetta picked up a green bean, snapped the ends off and dropped them in a trash sack. She broke the bean into thirds and put it in the large colander. She continued snapping beans and snatching frequent glances at the car until a man stepped out of the vehicle. Rhetta's gaze moved over him in a leisurely inspection. He was still unaware of her.

He was a tall man, easily six feet, with thick, shiny black hair and unruly curls that blew a little in the breeze. He wore sunglasses and khaki-colored shirt and pants, the type a big-game hunter might wear. His skin was tanned in a rugged sort of way, as though darkened by long hours of exposure to wind and sun while working, rather than while sunning lazily by a swimming pool. He stretched when he got out, arms way up high over his head, hands fisted, his leanly muscled body comfortable and relaxed beneath his clothes. His gaze strayed to the porch, and he smiled at them. A wave of sheer sensuality curled in the pit of Rhetta's stomach at his smile.

The man strolled down the sidewalk and up the gray porch steps, which needed painting again this year. Rhetta sat up a little straighter, warily, like a dog whose turf is being invaded. The man removed his sunglasses.

"It's me, Aunt Nanny. I'm home!"

"Land sakes! Bates! I didn't even recognize you. Come here and give your Aunt Nanny a great big hug." Bates loomed over the tiny woman and picked her up in a bear hug that lifted her sensible black orthopedic sandals clean off the floor. The green beans in her lap spilled unheeded onto the porch.

Rhetta's jaw dropped open and then snapped quickly shut again. Bates McCabe!

Bates McCabe had been reared in the Tucker Boarding House by Nanny, his maiden aunt, but by the time Rhetta was out of pigtails, he was hardened in the West Texas oil fields. Bates's parents had been killed in a car crash, and he'd come to live with them the year Rhetta turned four.

By the time Rhetta was ten, she was singing Bates's name in jump-rope songs as her one true love. At twelve, she was scrawling his name on the secret back pages of her notebook and weaving girlish fantasies about the wild and exciting teenager Bates had become.

All the older girls in Tuckerville had been crazy about Bates, but Rhetta had always believed she was special to him.

He'd race out the front door of the boarding house on sleepy summer afternoons and stop in midstride as he spied Rhetta and Janie Lou Perkins playing jacks in the shade of the front porch. He'd stroll up to them and tug Rhetta's ponytail. "Rhetta Tucker," he'd say, "when are you going to grow up so I can marry you? A fellah can't wait forever, you know."

Rhetta was thirteen when Bates graduated from high school and then attended Rice University. Rhetta moped about the boarding house for months and sang heartrending songs of unrequited love, feeling a womanly martyrdom far beyond her years. Bates had filled her teenage fantasies for as long as she could remember; she'd always known that Bates McCabe was her one and only.

Bates left Rice after two years to become a roughneck in the oil fields. Nanny had gone to visit him several times in various cities through the years, but Bates had never come back to Tuckerville, and like most teenage crushes, Rhetta's died a long and painful death. Now he was back.

Rhetta watched as Bates lowered Nanny back to the floor, then placed both hands on her shoulders. He looked down at Nanny with a deep affection that made Rhetta feel warm.

He had always seemed big to Rhetta, but now he seemed even bigger—more manly. His shoulders were broad and muscular, his legs, long and straight. But there was something more; he was, well, sexy, Rhetta thought without embarrassment at her assessment. Swarthy and reckless, hair curling riotously and such a powerful build. Why there wasn't a man in all of Tuckerville who could compare with the physical power she sensed as she watched Bates embrace Nanny.

"And who's this?" he asked as he stared down at Rhetta with interest.

Rhetta straightened into a more alert position, and her lips curved into a polite smile.

"Well, don't you recognize her? This is Ellen and Poog's daughter, Rhetta," Nanny admonished.

"So," he said softly, "you've grown up, Rhetta."

Rhetta's stomach dropped and her heart seemed to beat erratically at his words. A familiar, almost painful longing stirred deep within her heart. "Stand up and let me look at you." His voice was silky and husky and commanding all at the same time. Rhetta stood up.

"Well, I know I've changed a little since I was twelve." Rhetta felt self-conscious, more like the girl she'd been when she'd first started developing a figure than like a woman of twenty-eight. Her breasts were full, and the material of the strawberry cotton dress outlined their shape. A matching belt cinched in her waist, and her hips were merely suggested by the draping material. She was, her mother had often said, full figured. Rounded in all the right places. His eyes roamed her body, as if he were her lover, and she felt a tingling sensation ripple along her nerve ends.

Rhetta looked down at her bare feet. Bates was looking at her feet, too, with a lopsided grin on his face. Rhetta wiggled her toes as if in greeting. His grin widened as he looked up and met her eyes.

"I believe I'd recognize those bare feet anywhere." Bates laughed, and Rhetta and Nanny joined in.

"I don't sport nearly as many skinned knees as I did back then, and the only cut fingers I have now are a result of carelessness while I'm slicing up the vegetables for dinner." Rhetta smiled and picked up the colander. "Nanny, why don't y'all go into the parlor and sit where it's a bit cooler while I finish these green beans."

"Oh, just look at the mess I've made!" Nanny spied the green beans scattered all over the gray floor and moved to pick them up.

"Don't you dare, Nanny Fields. How many years have you been waiting for Bates to come back here? And when he finally has, you are *not* going to start working," Rhetta said firmly.

"Well, all right." Nanny acquiesced quite easily for Nanny. She was clearly too pleased by Bates's unexpected return to protest much. Nanny turned, and Rhetta watched her take Bates by the arm to escort him inside. He was certainly all man, Rhetta thought, and smiled to herself.

As Nanny preceded him through the door, Bates turned and caught Rhetta, still poised with the colander in her hand, staring at him. His gaze perused her figure with approval, and as his eyes moved up to her face, he smiled, more with his eyes than his mouth. Silently he sent a message that said he promised to see her later.

Rhetta turned away without returning his look, her expression closed and guarded, and bent silently to pick up the spilled beans and trash sack.

She was not going to waste her adult years the way she had her adolescence, mooning over a vagabond fantasy lover whose reputation as a wild ladies' man probably did not exceed actuality. Rhetta made it a rule never to become involved with guests just passing through, and as far as she was concerned, Bates McCabe fit that category comfortably.

Slipping her shoes back on, she opened the screen door with one hand and, once inside, kept it from slamming by easing it shut with her foot. She looked briefly into the parlor when she entered, meeting Bates's knowing look with a steady stare that gave no quarter. Turning left, she moved away from the parlor and into the dining room and then through the white swinging door into the kitchen.

She slipped off her shoes, kicked them under the chopping table and grabbed an old apron from the hook behind the door.

It was still the same, she thought as she shoved the colander under the faucet to rinse the snap beans. The instant attraction she'd always felt toward Bates was still there. Except now that skin-tingling magic she'd felt as an adolescent had blossomed into a woman's desire.

There was a difference. Bates returned the attraction. Rhetta could feel it; she could almost taste it.

It was a chilling discovery for her to realize that rational thought played no part in the primal call that Bates exuded. Rhetta's response was no less instinctual, but she could and would control her reaction.

Rhetta sighed and shook her head. The evening breeze lifted the curtains on the kitchen window. Rhetta liked the way the breeze carried a clean, fresh smell to her as she finished snapping the beans. She could recall a boy quite different from the man she'd seen today.

She remembered her mother and Nanny shaking their heads in unison because he'd made a date with one girl for seven o'clock and with a different girl for nine o'clock. And she remembered the time he'd gotten a job at T. Johnson's Fountain and Druggery and ate his whole week's wages in three days.

Rhetta turned and dumped the beans into the pot on the stove. The salt pork in the boiling water made the steam smell good and would give strength and a good flavor to the beans. Rhetta opened the oven, pulled the chicken out and turned the pieces over so that they would all be baked and browned evenly. After checking the rice and rolls, she went into the dining room to set the table for dinner.

"Oh, Rhetta, we were just coming to find you. Bates wants to take that extra room tonight."

"You do have a room?" Bates interjected. "You probably have a lot of visitors come through this exciting town, don't you?" he added, teasing.

Rhetta was irritated by his manner. Perhaps it was because, as mayor of Tuckerville, she'd worked so hard trying to bring new business into the town to make it grow. Or perhaps she wanted to dislike him; anger seemed a sturdy barrier to other emotions.

"We do have a few out-of-town guests now and again," Rhetta said stiffly. She kept her eyes down and placed a white napkin beside a fork. "Although not quite as many as Houston or Dallas."

Comparing Tuckerville to Houston was ludicrous. Rhetta wished she could take the words back as soon as she'd said them. His mouth pulled down at one corner, as if he was mocking her statement. Rhetta tightened her jaw.

"Oh, yes, that's right," Nanny offered, sensing Rhetta's defensiveness. "We did have that shoe salesman down from Jasper last year who was sweet on you and then that big-shot lumber man over from Tupelo." Nanny turned to Bates and added, "He was sweet on her too."

Rhetta wished Nanny hadn't said anything at all. She knew the other woman was only trying to help, but Nanny had made things sound worse than ever. While Tuckerville might not be completely dead, it wasn't exactly in the fast lane, either. But the town suited Rhetta just fine. She didn't meet Bates's gaze, even though she could feel the weight of his stare.

"So all the men who come to stay here are sweet on you?" Bates's eyes were teasing when Rhetta looked up at him. She smiled slightly and continued moving around the long table, laying the place settings.

"No, they just—"

"Rhetta could have her pick of men," Nanny interrupted. "Any one of the boys around here would be more than happy to marry her. But she'll have none of them. She's had more marriage proposals than any woman I know. She turns them all down." Looking proudly at Rhetta, Nanny smiled.

Rhetta knew Nanny was proud of her, but sometimes she just wished Nanny would keep her pride to herself. Bates was staring at Rhetta like a dog at dinnertime—as though she was his for the asking. Rhetta knew that if she looked up at him, he'd be grinning. She felt defensive and angry and she didn't even know why.

"Nanny, why don't you take Bates up and show him his room," she said tersely. "You know where the key is." Rhetta didn't even look at them when she spoke. Instead, she smoothed imaginary wrinkles from the napkins and tablecloth.

"All right, dear," Nanny said, and Rhetta could tell Nanny was wondering what she had done to offend her. Nanny gingerly walked out of the dining room, as if Rhetta might lash out at her like a crazy woman for making too much noise.

Rhetta didn't have to look up to see that Bates had stayed. He leaned down over her as she continued pretending to be preoccupied with smoothing out the napkins.

"I didn't mean to upset you," he said quietly.

"You didn't. I—oh." Rhetta let out a soft sigh of frustration, more with herself than with him. "You did, but it wasn't you. It was me. I'm just touchy." Rhetta looked up at him, and he cocked his head to one side, waiting for further explanation. "Everyone talks as if Tuckerville is dead and nothing ever happens here. But things do happen here. Maybe people don't get shot here and companies don't negotiate million-dollar business deals or strike million-dollar oil wells, but things *do* happen here. Important things.''

Rhetta picked up a fork and shined it with a napkin even though it didn't need shining. After a moment of silence, she continued, ''We got the bank lobby recarpeted, Mary Louise Hopkins taught old Timber how to read after fifty years, Lucille Beckett lost two teeth in three days and Jonas Neal donated the use of his land for the church picnic. Now I know those things won't set the world on fire with excitement, but they're important because they're about people— people who care about one another and help and... Oh, I guess I'm just tired,'' Rhetta said softly. She had to offer some excuse for her irritability. It all sounded so stupid and petty next to the things that went on in Houston. In Tuckerville, no oil tankers blew up and no airplanes crashed. The people made Tuckerville what it was.

''I think it's good to have pride in Tuckerville,'' Bates said reflectively. ''It's a place where you can feel that you belong. And most people don't feel that way in Houston. You're right. It is the people that make any town dead or alive.'' His voice had lowered to a soft, husky pitch that hypnotized Rhetta with its seductive quality. ''It's the caring that makes the difference. And I suppose I've always believed Tuckerville was rich in that respect. Maybe that's why I've come back,'' he mused.

Rhetta stood still. The curtains lifted gently as the breeze pushed through the window, bringing the scent of the pine trees on its breath. Her auburn hair tickled her skin when it brushed along her shoulders as she stood staring off into space, as if in a trance. She could feel his stare but couldn't tear her gaze away from the window, couldn't tear herself away from her thoughts.

Bates moved closer and Rhetta looked up at him. His deep tan made the hollows beneath his cheekbones darker, and the stubble of his beard gave him a swarthy, reckless appearance. The first two buttons of his shirt were open, exposing the perspiration that streaked down his throat in rivulets and stained the khaki material of his shirt to a darker shade.

He was earthy and masculine, a tangible force that evoked a desire in Rhetta that she did not name, that she would not name. There was a questioning heat in the depths of his blue eyes that made Rhetta's stomach lurch suddenly.

"What are you thinking?" he asked softly.

It would sound silly to say she had been thinking of the way the sunlight turned his hair to an almost liquid black or to say that his voice had the soothing, resonant quality of a Peggy Lee record played in the morning. It would sound silly to say that more than anything else she wished they were walking down Kern's Hill to sit in the shade of the pine trees and then lie down together on a bed of soft pine needles and let the cool air dry the sweat on their skin. It would sound silly, but more than that, it would be revealing.

Giving him a tight smile, Rhetta mutely shook her head.

Bates reached up to touch her face then, but Rhetta pulled back as Nanny walked in.

"Come on, Bates," Nanny ordered. "We've got to get you settled in so I can help Rhetta serve. Dinner's got to be served at six o'clock sharp," she warned.

For a moment Bates stayed where he was. Rhetta lowered her gaze, turned and went into the kitchen, leaving the white door swinging on its hinges.

After the six boarders ate dinner, Nanny and Rhetta washed the dishes. Then Nanny went upstairs to read before bed, and Rhetta went out to sit on the front porch to be alone. Just like always.

It was quiet outside at the end of a working day. After washing the dishes in hot, steamy water, the breeze felt cool against her skin. The moon was a tiny sliver of silver in the black Texas sky. A few stars were out, but they seemed so far away that their twinkling seemed very faint, almost like Tinkerbell when she is about to die.

Rhetta sighed and sat down on the wooden porch rail so that her body formed an L. Her back rested against one white porch column and the tips of her toes touched another.

She gazed out at the darkness of the night until even the friendly sound of crickets chirping sounded melancholy. Rhetta wanted to put on a Billie Holiday record and listen to it all by herself, but it was hard to listen to the blues with six other people listening, too.

The only record player she had was in the parlor, and everyone except Nanny congregated in there at night. The parlor had an air conditioner, and it was the only room that was cool and had a television set.

Rhetta sighed. She looked down at her feet. She was barefoot again. She must have left her shoes in the kitchen, but she just couldn't face going back in the house when the night air felt so cool and inviting on her skin. She shifted her back along the column until she found a comfortable spot to lean against.

The conversation earlier in the afternoon with Bates had left her more upset than she'd realized. She felt tired and lonely and sad, like a prisoner who knows there's no parole, no hope.

Rhetta wanted to run away. From everything and everyone. She was tired, bone tired. She worked so hard seven days a week, yet it seemed as if she never got caught up on anything. She wanted to forget Tuckerville, forget her idiotic promise to her father, forget that her ancestors ever founded this dying town. She tilted her head so that her auburn hair shielded her face.

"Mind if I join you?" Bates stepped from the shadows.

Rhetta lifted her head and turned to look at him. She didn't want company. She didn't want him to see that she was feeling sorry for herself, even if she was.

"Last time I saw you, you were—what? Ten or eleven?" he asked companionably. His shoes made hollow thumping sounds as he came closer.

"I was thirteen years old, and you left in August. Everyone always leaves in August," Rhetta said dully. She turned away from him and looked out at the night. Yellow porch lights and twinkling blue stars dotted the darkness.

"Who's everyone?"

"Everyone who's ever come to live here. They all leave, and pretty soon the only people left in this town are going to be Nanny and me. And then I'll have to leave because I won't be able to survive without my boarders and my position at the library." Rhetta felt like crying.

"Oh, come on. It can't be that bad. This afternoon you assured me this town was bustling with activity."

Rhetta rolled her blue eyes heavenward and shrugged. "I just said it wasn't dead—yet."

"You've still got time. After all, you *are* the mayor." Bates propped his foot near Rhetta on a low rung of the porch railing.

"If you're talking about advertising to attract new businesses, I've already tried that. I sent out notices and offers to all the towns around here and got nothing. No responses. Not one. I've tried everything I know how to do." A frog croaked contentedly from under the porch and stopped when Bates spoke again.

"How long have you been mayor?" Bates's forearm rested casually on his thigh.

"Three years. I was elected mayor right before Mama died."

"Well, what have you done to try to improve Tuckerville? This can be your state-of-the-town speech." He grinned at her, trying to lift her drooping spirits.

"Everything. I printed brochures and sent them out—but they didn't look too nice because I don't really have a budget and Harley's Print Shop doesn't have a way to do color." Rhetta shrugged. "I wrote letters to all the businesses in the area and called on people. The fact is nobody wants to risk opening a major business here and then a year later have trouble getting workers because the town's folded up. Most of the people left in Tuckerville are Nanny's age," Rhetta reported dismally.

"Yeah, there's always been an abundance of gray heads around here." Bates smiled at her gently, and Rhetta's spirits rose a little. "Why do you suppose the businesses think the town will fold? It's been poking along all right for the last thirty years."

Rhetta swiveled so that her legs hung off the railing and she faced him. "But that's just it, Bates—it's been poking. People die here all the time, but they aren't born here very often. Our population drops little by little every year. A businessman looks at our population statistics and decides he'd rather build in a larger, more prosperous town."

"Why do people stay here? Why do *you* stay in Tuckerville? There must be something that keeps you here besides your heritage." Bates gestured at the street, and suddenly Rhetta knew what kept her here, what kept them all here.

Rhetta stayed because Mary Lou Simpkins made the best pineapple turnovers in the whole world, because the old man in the gray painted house on Third Street would still shine shoes for twenty-five cents and would give folks all the tomatoes they wanted for free. And when the sun became hotter, there was hand-turned ice cream on Willie Dale's porch, Louise's blue-ribbon peach cobbler and catfish for everyone when Sammy had a good day at the lake. Summertime meant inner tubes that gave anybody who slid off them wrong a raw stomach, rides in leaky rowboats in cool violet twilights, sunburned noses on Monday and marathon Monopoly games on rainy Sunday afternoons.

Rhetta stayed for the quiet of the woods in the fall when the air was a bit crisper, for the smell of pine logs burning, for wheelbarrow races in red sweatshirts and blue jeans, for Saturday leaf raking and Wednesday bread baking, for long walks on long afternoons all by herself.

Rhetta stayed because Mrs. Heimer still read *Pride and Prejudice* to the girls and *Robinson Crusoe* to the boys until her voice gave way and because Mr. Stevens still dressed up like a ghost when he gave out sticky candy on Halloween. And most of all, Rhetta stayed because the woods smelled so clean and fresh, and the moonlight shone on the winding path just right for midnight strolls.

Rhetta cleared her throat and looked away from her memories.

"I guess I've stayed here because I really couldn't imagine calling anyplace home except Tucker Boarding House...." Rhetta wanted to say more, to tell him about her thoughts, but she couldn't quite share that with him. Not yet.

"Yeah, I know," Bates said softly, and ruffled her hair a bit before he took a deep breath and looked out at the familiar town where he, too, had come of age.

Suddenly Rhetta believed Bates did know why she had stayed when all of her friends had moved away to Shreveport or Dallas or Beaumont or Houston.

It wasn't that she lacked ambition, because she didn't. But Rhetta had dreamed of making Tuckerville grow and prosper since she was a little girl. As mayor, Rhetta worked hard, but she knew that attracting stable manufacturing operations to Tuckerville was a long and arduous process.

"Maybe I could help you and Tuckerville out a little bit," he offered.

"How?" Rhetta leaned her head to one side as she peered up at him in the moonlight.

"Well, in a sense, the government subsidizes businesses that come to small towns like Tuckerville and set up manufacturing operations. The businesses are willing because it's cheaper for them to operate a manufacturing concern in a small out-of-the-way town like Tuckerville and because they get a tax break. Everybody wins." Bates shrugged his broad shoulders and smiled.

"I'm familiar with that program, and I've been working with Sarah Long to expand her business. She designs and sews baby clothes. But when Sarah applied, they turned her down because she was asking for too much money. I suppose that Sarah's business was too small and untried for them to loan her money for constructing a whole building."

"I don't know. Maybe you didn't ask the right people. But I've researched it all pretty carefully. Has Sarah thought about using one of the many available buildings around town? Word has it that Justus Burns will lease or sell quite cheaply.''

''Really? He must be getting senile. He's so tight he—''

''Squeaks when he walks. How many times have you heard Nanny say that about him?''

''Plenty of times.'' They laughed softly together and then became quiet. Rhetta felt relaxed and contented.

She looked at Bates and felt that familiar yearning of her teenage years come creeping back. She was surprised by the strength of the attraction she felt toward him. It was the powerful kind, the kind of feeling that made her stomach sink and her heart start pounding just because he smiled a certain way.

She paused then, pushing her wayward thoughts aside and trying to concentrate on what he had said regarding Sarah's baby-clothing business.

''Do you really think that Sarah could get some money from the government if she used one of the old buildings around here?'' Rhetta asked, feeling a bit more hopeful.

''It might be a whole lot easier. Give Senator Hawkins a call and ask him what could be done,'' Bates suggested. ''I'm sure he'd be willing to help you.''

''I'll do that.'' Suddenly Rhetta was excited. Excited about Tuckerville, excited about Sarah's baby-clothing business and excited, too, because Bates was home. With her. ''Oh, I could just—'' Rhetta clapped both hands over her mouth. She had been about to say she could kiss him.

"You could what?" He grinned at her, as if he knew what she'd been about to say, and Rhetta colored faintly. He circled her wrist with his fingers.

Rhetta looked down at his hand around her wrist and then looked knowingly up at him. He smiled with one side of his mouth and tugged gently at her wrist. She'd been wanting him to kiss her since she'd first seen him today, and now he would. Rhetta stood up and let herself be drawn into his arms.

At their first contact, Rhetta knew it would be good. Her breasts were crushed softly against his chest, and she could feel his belt buckle pressing into the soft flesh of her stomach. He tunneled his hand underneath her hair and with his thumb pressed her chin up. Hoping the real thing would taste as sweet as in her imagination, Rhetta lifted her head, and their lips met with soft, sweet hesitancy.

He rolled his lips across hers and nipped softly at her lower one. Shivering, she gloried in the feel of his soft lips and in his rough callused hand, stroking her arm. Bates lifted his head and rubbed his thumb across her lips, as if he were testing to see if they were real.

Rhetta burrowed her head into his chest, snuggling closer and enjoying the feeling of his warm, hard-muscled body. Bates rubbed his hand in circular motions over her back. She sighed in contentment. They remained silent for a moment, enjoying the feel of each other's body. Then Rhetta's mind returned to their conversation about Tuckerville.

"What we really need to find is someone who would put a large manufacturing plant here." She ran her glossy pink fingernail down the opening of his shirt and raised her head to look at him.

"Well, what about me?" he asked, and pulled her closer against him, so that she could feel his chest expand with every breath he took.

"You? You don't have a business. I thought you were a roustabout."

"I was until a couple of years ago. Then I got hooked on computers. I want to start a manufacturing business here. I know it will work. It'll take off like a—"

Rhetta pushed out of his arms. The last man who had tried this on her she'd pushed down the porch steps.

"Hey!" he said, his black brows rushing together.

"And all you need to start up your little boom business is a lot of cash from our bank, right?" she asked acidly.

"Well, of course I need—" He couldn't imagine what was wrong with her.

"Don't you think we've had offers like yours before?" she interrupted scathingly, taking no notice of his eyes as they narrowed. "What did you think? That you could stroll right into this Podunk town and take a free ride? Engage in a little post office on the side with the local mayor? Seduce me so that I'd pull a few strings for you? Is that it?"

He grabbed her so quickly that Rhetta didn't even have a chance to back away. She hadn't even seen him move. He shoved her back flat against the porch column and held her there.

"Who I kiss has nothing to do with their position in life or lack of it," he said derisively. "You may think you own this town, but you don't. Oh, I know all about how your high-and-mighty ancestors founded this town and that now you're the queen bee and ready to take charge. But you haven't. You've been mayor for three years, and your mother was mayor for ten years before that, and neither one of you know anything about business. It's no wonder the town's gone steadily downhill. You should get down on your knees and thank God I'm even considering Tuckerville. I've had plenty of offers and I'll probably end up taking one of them. But if nothing else, you should at least consider the jobs the computer industry would bring to this town."

"The computer industry is just like the oil industry." Rhetta crossed her arms and planted her feet firmly. "Up one year and down the next. A town like Tuckerville can't take the yo-yo effect of that type of business. That's why Tuckerville is dying today. Too much of our economy depended on the oil business and that's been drying up around here since 1930, when it started. We don't need the likes of you sending our town into orbit with a crummy computer business that will leave us worse off than before." Rhetta tried to jerk away from him, but he pushed her back against the column again.

"And just what kind of business do you want to bring to this town? Huh?" He jabbed a finger at her, and Rhetta's temper rose even higher.

"A cotton mill would be just fine with me!" she shouted. Rhetta lowered her voice when she realized how high it had risen. "Or a lumber mill. There are scads of tree farms around here."

"Yeah, and there are scads of lumber mills around here, too," he stated pointedly. "Your problem is that you only see what's right in front of your face. Tuckerville. Have you ever been outside this town? There's a world out there, Rhetta," he said, stepping back and waving his arm toward the street, "and it has a lot more to offer than what's right here in Tuckerville."

This time when she jerked away from him, he let her go. As she stomped across the porch to the front door, the thought occurred to Rhetta that it was very difficult to be dignified with bare feet.

Bates watched her walk into the house and then turned and looked out at the night. Somebody's dog was barking in the neighborhood, and someone hollered at it to stop. Bates ran his fingers through his hair and then drummed on the wooden rail.

He lifted his hand and leaned against the wooden column where Rhetta had stood a few moments ago.

What had gotten into her? he wondered, amazed. One minute she was purring contentedly, and the next she was screaming like a Fury. Damn!

It was hard for him to reconcile the two images he had of her. One was of a pigtailed tomboy with pale blue eyes and bandages on her knees, chin and elbows. The other was of an auburn-haired seductress who had a tendency to play it safe and who hadn't even explored the full potency of her sexual charms.

She'd gotten under his skin the first minute he'd laid eyes on her. There was something so sultry and unconsciously sensual in her every move that Bates had been aroused just watching her snap the damned beans. She was a full-blooded woman, all right, but not in the sex-siren way; she was too reserved, too conservative for that. But the heat was there waiting for one man and one man only. Bates had known that the first second he'd seen her.

But why was she so damned conservative! Bates turned away and looked at the door she had gone through and then back out at the night again. He shoved his hands deep into the pockets of his trousers.

She had a cookie-jar mentality. Rhetta was the type who put all of her money into savings, cutting corners, never buying on credit. He was the type who took risks, gambled—he played for the high stakes.

Bates placed one foot on the porch rail and leaned over so that his arm rested on the column. She didn't recognize that in order to make money, you had to spend it, he thought. The days were gone when a town could live on farming or natural resources alone. Tuckerville had to diversify, keep up with the times and bring in new technology, new industries that had a solid future. A town had to take chances, risks, in order to prosper. And taking risks was what Bates did best.

Rhetta had good intentions but she didn't have an ounce of business sense. Under her style of leadership, Tuckerville would poke along and stay a two-horse town and finally fizzle out twenty years from now. On the other hand, if they would take a chance on him, he knew he could make this town really start buzzing. He could bring this town to life.

Bates breathed in deeply. His exasperation with Rhetta mixed with excitement as he thought about his project. It was a golden opportunity for him to revive this lovely old town and become a monumental success in business, as well.

It's not everyone who has the opportunity to revive a town, a people, a hope, and it's not everyone who gets to fulfill a boyhood fantasy, a dream of building a business from scratch and making it work, he thought as he stared out at the dim lights of Tuckerville. The odds were against him. He knew that. But he also knew that if determination and aggressiveness could make his plan succeed, it ought to be a booming success.

Bates smiled and rubbed his knuckles across his chin, liking the scratchy sound it made. She might be a tough opponent, but he'd always enjoyed a good struggle. It made the victory sweeter. Especially with women.

Chapter Two

Rhetta gulped down a cup of coffee, took two bites of a day-old donut and ran out the back door. She wanted to be out of the house before Bates or Nanny got up.

The dew was still shimmering on the grass, but Rhetta wasn't the first to leave footprints. Mrs. Bookerton's mongrel, Sir Francis Drake, so called because his tail reminded Minnie Bookerton of the plume Sir Francis Drake had worn in his hat, had visited Rhetta's petunia bed to bury its bone.

Rhetta shook her head at the destruction the dog had caused and then hurried down the cracked driveway to the sidewalk, where she slowed her pace.

Every day, Rhetta worked at the library from eight
o'clock until one o'clock and then shopped for gro-
ceries or went home to do laundry, garden, pick vegetables or clean before starting dinner for the
boarders. But today, Rhetta had other plans for her
afternoon.

Pausing at the only stoplight in town, Rhetta looked
both ways before she scurried across the street on a red
light. She looked back over her shoulder to see if anyone had seen her; it wouldn't set a good example for
anyone to see the mayor breaking the law.

Rhetta walked past the drug store and three old but
sturdy buildings that stood vacant and unkempt. Their
dirty windows needed a good cleaning, and the tall
weeds that poked up through the cracks in the sidewalk gave downtown Tuckerville a has-been look.

Rhetta always walked quickly by those three buildings, and this morning she walked even faster than
usual.

Faye Kern was sweeping the porch steps of her café,
her orange hair spilling over her face and highlighted
in the sunshine. Finishing the bottom step, she
rhythmically stroked the broom across the sidewalk.
She paused when she saw Rhetta coming, pushed her
hair up out of her face and leaned on her broom.
Rhetta stopped politely in front of her.

"Good morning, Mrs. Kern."

"Mornin' Mayor. But I don't know about how good
it is after what I heard last night," Faye said forebod-
ingly, shifting her substantial weight from one foot to

the other, as if her faded blue tennis shoes were too tight for her.

"What's that?" Rhetta asked, knowing that Faye had intended she ask.

"The Baggleys is movin' away," she said accusingly, making Rhetta feel guilty and somehow responsible. "They was one of my best customers. Most every Sunday after church they'd be up here eatin' the special."

"Why are they moving? I thought Jim Baggley got a job at the grocery mart." Rhetta's heart sank at the news, and her body seethed with impatience to get away and start on her plan.

"He got laid off. Business was too slow. Most folks have gardens in the summer, and that really cuts into the grocery business. You better do somethin' quick to put this town back on its feet again or you ain't gonna have a town left to mayor over," Faye said sourly. She turned her back on Rhetta and began sweeping again.

Rhetta hurried past her and crossed the street. Her footsteps echoed on Brick Street with a clackety-clack that lent an urgency to her mission.

She almost ran past the post office and began holding her side to stop it from aching, but still she kept moving. She went around the corner and halfway down the next block, until she reached the doors of the library. Her heart was pounding so hard that she stood outside a moment to still her shaking hands and catch her breath. She'd been running like a crazy woman— as though something was chasing her.

She took her keys out of her handbag, and they jingled noisily in the quiet Tuckerville morning. Rhetta looked behind her and then entered the library. Turning, she locked the door and walked straight into her office.

She checked the clock. It was not yet seven. That left her plenty of time to map out her strategy before she had to open the doors of the library. She'd show Mr. McCabe who was boss in this town.

Bates stretched his arms over his head and smiled as he came slowly awake. Today was his day. He rubbed the palm of his hand over the dark curly hairs on his chest and then locked his fingers behind his neck so that his arms stuck out like an eagle's wings, and yawned.

The cool white sheet was pushed down to his hips, but he could still smell their freshness. She must hang them outside to dry like her mother used to, he thought idly.

Bates smiled again. He had gotten her pretty angry last night. She was a good-looking woman but she was far too inexperienced to tackle a job like reviving an entire town. That took someone with authority and experience, he thought. Someone aggressive, gutsy— me.

Bates smiled at the idea of voicing those conceited thoughts to Rhetta and roared out loud when he thought how that would rile her. He was still smiling when he swung his feet over the side of the bed and glanced at the sunlight streaming in his window.

He rolled out of bed and tightened his muscles as he stretched the full length of his body in the golden sunlight. He felt strong. Ambitious. He'd had a dream—a dream so powerful and exciting that he felt as energetic as an eighteen-year-old. And all because of Rhetta Tucker.

He could no more resist teasing Rhetta than a dog could resist a bone. It was meant to be. The chemistry was there between them, and he knew they would be on opposite sides of the table until his plant was up and running. Then she'd come around. And he'd win. Everything.

Bates smiled and looked out the window of his bedroom. There she was, scurrying off as though she was running from a big black panther. She peeked over her shoulder and up at the house, as if she was nervous that he might be following her. He grinned and felt good that he'd been able to arouse her that much.

It must be later than he'd thought if she was already going off to work. He looked at the clock on the nightstand. Six-forty-five in the morning.

Bates's forehead knitted together in thought, and he rubbed his knuckles across his beard, making a scratchy, contemplative sound. What was she up to at six-forty-five in the morning? A small cloud appeared on the horizon of his future. Maybe he'd underestimated her, he thought with sudden wariness.

He'd better get a move on, or while he was still in the shower, she'd be a regular Paul Revere, alerting the whole town that he was trying to take over like some mobster. He knew women. They'd do anything to win. And Rhetta could probably rally the troops better than any general he'd ever known.

Bates remembered that the one shower for all six boarders was located down at the end of the long hallway. He'd better make a dash for it before everyone used up all the hot water.

Bates reached for the door handle, stepped outside his room and slammed the door behind him. He waited until he heard the lock click shut and then took a step forward. He stopped suddenly and looked down at himself. He was completely nude.

There was an added bounce to Rhetta's walk, an added lilt to her voice when she spoke to her library patrons. Pam Milton paid her fines, Jack Sims returned his books on time and Houston Terrel brought his little girl to the library.

The library had been Rhetta's first revival project. Before she became mayor, Tuckerville Library had been sitting idle for five years. Rhetta had single-handedly reopened it.

Rhetta's position as the sole librarian of Tuckerville Library was virtually voluntary, but it provided a welcome respite from the routine of the boarding house as well as intellectual stimulation.

By one o'clock Rhetta was humming to herself, and after she'd locked the doors to the library, she fairly skipped down the street to meet Sarah Long.

Rhetta met Sarah at the corner, and they greeted each other as they walked along the street.

Sarah Long was widowed, about forty, but because she had married young, her children were grown and gone to college or working in Dallas or Baton Rouge. Sarah had dark brown hair without a touch of gray and a seriousness about her that sat right with the people in Tuckerville.

Sarah operated her baby-clothing business out of her home. So far she had only one customer—a baby-clothes store in Pineland, but during the past few months, she and Rhetta had been working on getting orders from several stores in Dallas.

Rhetta had always liked the calm self-assurance Sarah exuded. Sarah's eyes, like her personality, were peaceful. Her voice was soft but commanded respect in Tuckerville.

"Rhetta, will you please answer me? Where are we going?" Sarah walked hurriedly beside Rhetta, skirting cracks in the sidewalk and broken glass.

"Are you still making baby clothes for that department store in Pineland?" Rhetta inquired, without slackening her pace.

"Yes," Sarah answered, obviously curious why Rhetta was asking.

"Do you remember when you said that children's store in Dallas called and wanted you to design and sew baby clothes for them?" Rhetta asked, still striding along the street purposefully.

"Yes, but I told them that I was too busy to do that and the sewing I'm doing now. I told them I'd call this fall. Now tell me what this is all about, or I won't go a step farther," Sarah threatened.

"You don't have to go a step farther. We're here." Rhetta stopped abruptly in front of the second of the three abandoned buildings downtown.

"So? It's the Thompson Building," Sarah said, squinting at the building in the sunlight and looking back at Rhetta.

"Soon this building will be called the Long Building," Rhetta said, and winked at Sarah as she unlocked the door.

"What are you talking about?" Sarah asked, puzzled.

Rhetta opened the door, then turned and pulled the key from the lock. As they both stepped inside, Rhetta noted the musty smell of the building. Old cardboard boxes, coat hangers and a nude female mannequin with one arm missing sat in a far corner of the room, next to what Rhetta presumed was a bathroom. The walls were painted industrial green and had large black scrapes in several places.

"I know we've talked for months on end about building a clothing-manufacturing plant next year, after we got your business built up a bit—" Rhetta twisted her fingers together nervously "—but, Sarah, I think the time is right."

"For what?" Sarah demanded, her patience wearing thin.

"For leasing the old Thompson Building as the new headquarters for Sarah's Baby Clothes Company," Rhetta said decisively. "I've talked to Justus Burns, and since property values are down in Tuckerville, he'll lease it to you for next to nothing.'' Rhetta didn't reveal where she'd originally heard that information.

Sarah pulled a dusty chair away from the wall, removed a tissue from her purse and, after dusting the seat off, sat down, dumbfounded. She sat quite still for a moment, absorbing this new idea. "Well, I don't know,'' she said breathlessly. "I'd never really thought about converting a downtown building into a clothing-manufacturing plant. I think I should make sure I can get the contract for the baby clothes from that children's store in Dallas.''

Rhetta tried a new tactic. "I've done some checking this morning and we can get the government to subsidize this manufacturing plant 'cause it will be so much cheaper than building one. I've already talked with Senator Hawkins's aide, and he's going to arrange it all for you. He's sending the forms and said there shouldn't be any trouble at all in obtaining the government grant after you know what your expenses will be.''

Rhetta could tell that Sarah thought she was simplifying complicated problems, but Rhetta felt that it could work if they tried hard enough.

"Oh, Rhetta. If only it were that simple." Sarah shook her head slowly.

"It is that simple. You've got a dirt-cheap location, the business and the right—''

"But, Rhetta,'' Sarah protested, "I've only got two places to sell clothes to and one's only a maybe. In order to open up a manufacturing operation, I'll need several chains of retail outlets to stock my merchandise."

"I'll tell you what, let's call Jim Hopkins over at the bank and tell him you'll be in at ten tomorrow morning. This afternoon let's phone around to some places in Dallas and see if we can't get some more customers for you. If we can't, we'll drive up there to show them some samples, and we won't commit to the Thompson Building until we get some more contracts. Fair enough?" Rhetta put her hands out, palms up in a gesture of appeal.

Rhetta watched as Sarah's eyes began to snap in anticipation as the idea took hold, and Rhetta knew Sarah was hooked.

"Fair enough. Oh, Rhetta..." Rhetta heard Sarah inhale deeply, and Rhetta's excitement was almost as great. "It'll need a lot of work to get this building in shape."

"Don't worry, I'll help you move in, and we can get someone to load your sewing machines and set them up here. How many do you have, anyway?" Rhetta paused, her hands on her hips, her head tilted in inquiry at Sarah.

"Five. Isn't that awful? A poor woman like me with five machines? It ought to be a sin. In fact, it might be a sin."

"Well, it also might be a blessing. After those phone calls we're going to make today and the orders you already have, you may have to deliver five hundred and fifty dresses over the next three months. And if you're going to market your line this fall, you'll need to hire a couple of seamstresses to help get the orders out so that you can be free to design new fashions." She saw that Sarah was a little overwhelmed. "Come on, I'm starving. Let's go get some lunch."

They walked down to the café, and Faye greeted them with a grumbly "afternoon" and took their orders before she seated them because the kitchen was about to close up for lunch.

Rhetta asked for a secluded table. Faye eyed Rhetta's jovial smile suspiciously and seated them at a table right next to the kitchen.

Probably so the old busybody can listen in, Rhetta thought.

Faye placed their orders in front of them with a loud clatter. "Tuna. Roast beef. Anything else?" She paused and looked at them.

"No, thank you, Faye. This is just wonderful!" Sarah exclaimed.

One corner of Faye's mouth lifted in what might be called a smile, for Faye.

Sarah and Rhetta exchanged conspiratorial looks before Faye left and then exchanged plates so that they had the correct order.

"We'll knock their socks off when we spring this on them at the town meeting tomorrow night," Rhetta said excitedly, thinking of the stunned expression that would be on Bates's face when he found out about her doings.

"We're having a town meeting about this tomorrow night?" Sarah asked incredulously.

"Well, not exactly." Rhetta pulled a corner of the bread crust off and waved her hand through the air evasively and then popped the scrap into her mouth. "The meeting is going to be over this government issue, and also Bates McCabe wants to open a computer-manufacturing plant in Tuckerville. Can you imagine? He wants our bank to loan him the money to do it," Rhetta said scathingly and rolled her blue eyes heavenward. She picked up her tuna sandwich and took a bite.

"When did he come back into town?" Sarah asked, noncommittally. "I thought he was out in West Texas working in the oil fields."

Someone punched an old Simon and Garfunkel tune on the juke box, and the soft chords filled the air as the diners from the lunch rush trickled out.

"He came back yesterday. And now he's into computers. He just seems to flit from one kind of boom business to another." Rhetta gestured airily with her hand and then placed both hands in her lap. "When one industry busts, he switches to the next, but this time he wants to take Tuckerville down with him. I'm going to fight him," Rhetta promised, her blue eyes gleaming at the challenge.

Sarah said nothing but raised her eyebrows slightly and continued eating.

"Now," Rhetta said, and scooted her chair up closer to the table, "I want you to help *me*. Would you call Steven Sutphen and ask him if he's still considering opening that tool-manufacturing plant? Tell him about the government subsidizing plan." Rhetta watched Sarah press her back against the chair and shake her head.

"He probably already knows about the plan, and no," Sarah said firmly, "I will not call him. You know what happened the last time I saw him. He went crazy. Told me he's loved me since high school and all that hogwash. Scared the daylights out of me." Sarah waved a dismissive hand at Rhetta, then smiled girlishly, nearly blushing in spite of herself. Her smile wasn't overlooked by Rhetta.

"Sarah. You owe me this. I need something big to present at the meeting, and Sutphen's plans are big. I'll bet he could hire twenty people or more with that operation he's been talking about. It could mean jobs and money for people, Sarah. For Tuckerville? For me? Please?" she wheedled.

Sarah looked at Rhetta, and Rhetta knew Sarah was seeing her as the little girl she once was, always begging for another donut at the bakery.

"Oh, all right," Sarah said, giving in with a smile, "I'll call him. If he's available, we'll meet him after dinner tonight. But Rhetta—" Sarah raised a warning finger.

"Yes?"

"Don't leave me alone with him for one second, okay?"

Bates looked out over the land surrounding the abandoned warehouse and breathed in the scent of the pines in the morning air. As far as the eye could see there were pine trees. *I've been away too long,* he thought with a sudden rush of nostalgic fondness for his boyhood home.

"Bates, come on over here and take a look at what Justus is showing you," Nanny shouted.

Bates expelled a short burst of laughter. *She always treats me like I was twelve,* he thought, and shook his head.

"All right," Bates answered, and moved to where Justus Burns and Nanny stood at the entrance of the cement warehouse.

Nanny wore a summer cotton flowered dress, but even so, there was still a hint of iron in the way she looked. Perhaps it was the orthopedic shoes she always sported or the way her white straw hat was formidably anchored to her gray curls. Whatever it was, it had been enough to keep Bates in line as a boy, which had been no easy task, if his memory served him correctly.

Justus Burns wore blue-and-white seersucker slacks, with white tennis shoes and a white straw hat with a red-and-navy band around the brim. Justus was half-a-head shorter than Aunt Nanny and had fat red cheeks that turned nearly purple when he smiled broadly. He limped slightly because of "an old war wound" that Aunt Nanny had secretly told Bates was from shooting himself in the foot with his daddy's pistol when he was a boy.

Justus was the only lawyer in Tuckerville, and as such, his status in the community was high. Besides, he owned about half the real estate in Tuckerville.

"I thought you'd like to be here when I opened her up," Justus said, and winked at Bates, as though he were still the freckle-faced youngster who used to sit on Justus's lap at his office in the courthouse.

Justus Burns had been courting Aunt Nanny for as long as Bates could remember, and they hadn't gotten any closer to tying the knot than when Bates had been a child. And from what Bates could see, they both liked it that way. Sweet romance between two of the most fastidious people he'd ever known. They'd drive each other crazy in a week if they ever got it in their heads to get married.

Justus pushed the door open, and the hinges creaked, more from lack of use than anything else, Bates thought. He knocked down a cobweb and scooted a dead grasshopper out of the way with the toe of his boot so that his aunt could pass through. Then he stepped inside and looked around. Justus followed, taking off his hat as he entered.

Bates felt a tingling down in the pit of his gut like he used to get when he was a kid playing hide-and-seek and knew someone was near, even though he hadn't heard them. It was a good omen.

"It needs a good cleanin'," Nanny admonished.

Bates grinned at her comment. Same old Aunt Nanny. He took a few steps forward to stand in the center of the room.

"Hello!" he shouted and his echo reverberated in the emptiness of the building.

"Got a good sound to her, doesn't she?" Justus offered, grinning. He limped forward to stand beside

Bates, and the uneven rhythm of his footsteps echoed against the walls.

"Mmmm," Bates answered noncommittally. After all, they hadn't yet begun to negotiate for the building.

He looked up at the ceiling. There didn't appear to be any leaks. A few minor cracks in the floor.

"How long has this been empty?" Bates put his hands on his hips and looked at Justus.

"Well, let's see. Joe Beggs built it. Built oil rigs. Then I bought it and leased it to Sandy Teller who... well, let's see, what did he use this building for, Nanny?" Justus Burns scratched his head. His black-rimmed glasses looked out-of-date and his eyes were magnified so that Bates thought they looked like two milky chocolate drops.

"Auto mechanics!" Nanny barked. "Can't you re-member that?" She looked over at Bates with arched eyebrows. "You'd think a man who thought the sun rose and set on his fancy Cadillac could remember Sandy Teller fixed cars in here," Nanny said point-edly. "It wasn't that long ago."

"It was too!" Justus boomed. "This warehouse has been empty for twenty years."

"Lord above! He's lost his marbles!" Nanny threw her hands heavenward and pursed her lips. "Are you gonna stand there and tell me I don't know my dates, Justus Burns?"

Their argument went on in this vein, but Bates tuned it out. He had heard too many of these exchanges to try to stop them or even to be bothered by them. In a strange way, this was how they showed their affection for one another. He went outside to walk the grounds and survey the building to make sure the foundation was solid.

Bates walked a straight line from the corner of the building out to the fence at the far end of the field, counting his paces as he went. This site was perfect for his plans. Enough parking and enough space for the expansion he'd need if his business took off the way he intended.

Bates had a good feeling about this venture. He knew his product, knew how to manufacture it at a reasonable cost and knew the market. All he needed was a start, so that he could gain the capital to really set the world afire with a new development he had already visualized. He was going to build his dream right here in this building, on this land. He was going to be an inventor.

Bates liked creating something from nothing. He liked molding and shaping. And that was another reason why he wanted to stay in Tuckerville. They needed him here. He could play a major role in revitalizing the town. It would be exciting building the town up and watching it grow. He knew it would be years until it would be safe to say Tuckerville was in the pink, but if he'd learned one thing from the oil business, it was tenacity. A man could never give up his dream; he had to stick it out no matter what.

Bates breathed in again and felt the fresh air of the country fill his lungs. His gaze traveled across the way to Kern's Hill and the unseen woods beyond. Pines, as tall as the eyes could see, one after another, their trunks sticky with resin, and the forest floor carpeted with golden pine needles and brown spiky pinecones. It was good to be back home.

Rhetta stood at the counter, beating the chocolate icing and humming to herself. The sun was setting on her second wonderful day in a row. Everything had gone just perfectly. Last night she and Sarah had talked Steven Sutphen into opening a machine-tool-manufacturing plant in Tuckerville instead of in a slightly bigger town down the road, as he had tentatively planned.

That he had agreed to build in Tuckerville was a miracle in itself, and the surprise announcement that he would move to Tuckerville and run the plant himself ensured its success.

Rhetta suspected that he had agreed to come to Tuckerville largely because of his affection for Sarah Long. He had been sweet on Sarah since they were in high school, and now that her husband had passed away, he obviously aimed to make his move.

This morning Sarah had leased the Thompson Building from Justus Burns for six months, practically for peanuts. And this very afternoon Sarah had made a verbal agreement to deliver two hundred and fifty dresses in two months to a Houston chain store. Things were happening quickly. Tuckerville hadn't seen this much action since Brady Jones's house caught fire five years ago.

"Do you want me to set the table for you?" Nanny paused at the kitchen door and looked at Rhetta.

"Would you? I'm hoping I can get out of here by seven, so I can be early to the town meeting." Rhetta turned on the burner beneath the skillet and waited for it to get hot. She sprinkled the pork chops with rosemary, salt and pepper and set them aside. Then she began icing the cake she'd made, stopping every so often to lick the creamy fudge icing from her fingertips.

Nanny came back into the kitchen and began washing the dishes Rhetta had used while preparing dinner.

"Bates coming to the meeting tonight?" Rhetta put the last swirl on the top of the cake, looked up at Nanny and back down again, not knowing how much Nanny knew about their heated exchange two days ago.

"I imagine so," Nanny said calmly. "He bought the warehouse east of town over by Kern's Hill. Signed the papers today."

Rhetta caught her breath. She had expected him to move quickly, but she hadn't been prepared for this! She pressed her teeth together so that her jaw felt locked and wiped her hands on the apron tied around her waist.

She tossed the pork chops into the skillet. Their hissing was oddly soothing to Rhetta as she contemplated her next move concerning Bates. She felt like hissing too.

Nanny busied herself wiping down the counters and getting out the iced tea and sugar.

"Rhetta?" Nanny's expression was concerned when she glanced at Rhetta.

"I'm all right, just a little stunned, that's all." Rhetta turned the pork chops over as the aromas of the rosemary and pork mingled together.

"I thought you'd be happy about this. I thought you wanted new businesses in Tuckerville."

"I do." Rhetta moved away from the stove, took the coleslaw out of the refrigerator and put it on the dining room table. "But I don't want boom businesses that don't have any stability moving into Tuckerville. A computer-manufacturing business will hire a bunch of people, and everyone will be happy for a while. But when the market goes sour, and it will—" Rhetta held up a fork in warning "—everyone will get laid off, and all the businesses built up during the boom will fold. More people will move away, and Tuckerville will no longer be. But if we slowly build up small businesses, we could stabilize Tuckerville, and maybe in a few years the town could support a big manufacturing operation like the one Bates wants. But not now. We aren't ready for it."

"I should think you'd want Bates to succeed," Nanny said sharply.

"I do want him to succeed, Nanny, but let him take his chances somewhere else, not in Tuckerville."

"Well, I can't believe you'd turn away your own kind just so you can still be queen over this town. Bates came here to help Tuckerville. I don't believe

your daddy would be very proud of you right now."
Nanny's lips were tightened in anger, and Rhetta hated
Bates even more for having come between her and
Nanny. Rhetta turned back to the stove.

"If you wouldn't mind, Nanny, please call everyone to eat," she said stiffly. Rhetta took the mashed
potatoes and carrots to the dining room table. She
wanted to steel herself for Bates's appearance. Last
night had been hard enough, but tonight was going to
be impossible. She banged the fork on the skillet in
frustration and seethed. "Damn!" she whispered
sharply.

When she heard the scraping of chairs being pulled
out and the good-natured chatter of the Miller twins,
Rhetta took a deep breath, removed her apron, picked
up the platter of pork chops and proceeded into the
dining room. After she placed the pork chops in front
of Douglas McFarland so that he could serve them,
Joey Heckenkemper stood up and pulled Rhetta's
chair out for her.

Forty-two years old, Joey Heckenkemper was the
youngest boarder, so everyone thought Rhetta and
Joey would get married eventually, even though
Rhetta had firmly kept their relationship at a just-
friends level for nearly four years.

After she was seated, Rhetta looked up and found
Bates seated directly across from her. He was staring
rather rudely at her. She met his gaze briefly before
lowering her head for the blessing.

"Thank you Lord for the bountiful blessings you
have bestowed upon us. Let us be thankful for one

another and let each heart be thankful for what you have given to him. Amen.''

"Amen,'' they intoned.

Douglas McFarland was a retired minister, so he always led the blessing and got to sit at the head of the table and serve the plates. Rhetta suspected that this sat sorely with Earl Miller, who felt that the men should take turns. Rhetta didn't want to hurt Mr. McFarland's feelings, so she let him continue.

After everyone's plate was served, Rhetta began eating. She avoided Bates's gaze and tried to concentrate on what Joey Heckenkemper was telling her.

"So anyway, they told me I had to pay a five-dollar fine for driving under the speed limit or appear in traffic court. I couldn't believe that such a thing could happen. So...'' Joey continued recounting his trip to Dallas, and Rhetta made interested murmurs.

She felt someone's foot brush hers. She had forgotten to put her shoes back on and was barefoot. She quickly tucked her feet closer to her chair so they wouldn't get stepped on.

She nodded to Joey but had no idea what he was telling her about. Again, something warm moved up her foot to her ankle, and this time there was no mistaking the implication. Or whose bare foot was rubbing hers.

Rhetta turned her head slowly, eyes glazed with anger, jaw clenched, and met his gaze. Bates smiled seductively at her, one side of his mouth pulled down in an almost challenging smile—as if he welcomed a battle with her.

Rhetta's fork was poised in midair, and as he stroked her foot, she felt the tension building between them. She longed to jerk her foot away, but she didn't because then he'd know that he could get to her. And Rhetta wanted him to think she was immune to him. Goose bumps prickled her leg, and Rhetta hoped he couldn't feel them. After all, two could play at this game.

Rhetta raised her eyebrows at him and then lowered her eyelids to a half-lidded, come-hither look. Slowly she let her fork rise to her mouth. She slid the mashed potatoes into her mouth and closed her lips around the fork. Then, still holding his gaze, she slowly slid the fork out and licked her full lips. She saw Bates swallow and his jaw go slack.

Rhetta hid her smile and watched him recover for a moment and then announced her departure.

"I've got to leave early for the meeting tonight. Nanny has agreed to serve you all the cake. So, I'll see everyone down there." She looked pointedly at Bates and he glared at her. Rhetta smiled smugly and ran upstairs to change her clothes.

Chapter Three

Rhetta folded her hands in her lap and then unfolded them. She stood up and smoothed the flared skirt of her wraparound dress back into place and smiled a little. She had selected the icy mint-green dress because she had read somewhere that cool colors kept people at a distance. And, oh, how she wanted to keep Bates at a distance. Preferably Siberia.

She had also worn the dress because she felt it accented her coloring; her auburn hair looked rich and thick against the pale jade color. And the cotton knit material of the dress gently molded her figure. She wanted to be alluring, and extremely distracting to Bates. She wanted to fluster him.

She glanced at her watch in agitation. It was twenty minutes after seven o'clock. She stood up and walked a few paces forward.

In one corner at the front of the room there was an American flag, and beside it, a Texas flag. A stained walnut lectern faced rows of steel folding chairs. And I'll be right up here, Rhetta thought as she ran a fingernail down a groove in the lectern.

When she heard the uneven rhythm of Justus Burns's gait coming down the hall, Rhetta turned to greet him. Because of all the gossip that got started here, Rhetta had always believed the court house had better acoustics than Carnegie Hall.

"Sorry, I'm a little late, Rhetta." Justus limped over to a folding chair and lowered himself into it. He sighed. "I'm just not as young as I used to be. Now," he said, scooting forward on the seat and hitching up his trouser legs, "what's this meeting all about?"

"Economic development."

"Mmm, now let me ask you again," Justus said pointedly. "What's this meeting all about?"

"Well, there's a lot been happening these past few days that I thought the town ought to be aware of," Rhetta said evasively as she sat down on the cold steel chair.

"Umm?"

"Yes, it's been really busy, and, well, I just thought the town ought to know all about it before it goes any further, that's all." Rhetta smoothed the material of her dress down over her knees and kept her eyes downcast.

Justus Burns had helped Rhetta get elected as mayor and was like a father to her. When she'd been growing up, Rhetta had always sought his advice on everything from ice-cream selection to dresses to wear to the prom. But she didn't know how Justus would feel about opposing Bates, because Bates had grown up in Tuckerville, too.

"Well?" he demanded. "Out with it. You're dying to tell me something and I'm ready to listen. So?" He sat back a little farther in his chair until it creaked.

"I don't want Bates to start his business here," Rhetta said bluntly. She met Justus's gaze squarely, and she thought she saw his brown eyes twinkle. It was hard to be sure, though, since his eyes were so magnified by his glasses.

"I figured as much."

"Well? Do you think I'm wrong?" she asked nervously.

"Rhetta, I'll admit that Bates has always been a bit of a wanderer and a gambler, but in this case it's not a matter of being right or wrong—it's a matter of what the people want."

"Well, what *do* the people want?" Rhetta asked, crossing her legs at the knees.

"They want jobs, Rhetta. And the merchants want more customers."

"Sarah's business will—"

"Sarah's business won't bring in many new customers or new folks to Tuckerville," he said brusquely. "Bates's business will. It will bring in young families, and that's what Tuckerville needs."

Rhetta could hear footsteps coming down the hall, and she knew her time to convince Justus Burns had ended. Rhetta pressed her lips together and stood up.

"Well, thank you for the advice." She met his eyes briefly, and it crossed her mind that Justus Burns looked tired.

As people filled the hall, Rhetta laid out her notes on the lectern. She smoothed her hair from her face and looked out at the audience, trying to establish some authority by standing at the lectern.

The audience at town meetings was usually composed of Tuckerville's business leaders, and tonight was no exception. Most of the merchants were there, but Rhetta hadn't caught sight of Bates yet. Maybe he chickened out, she thought sardonically.

Voices were raised in warm greetings, and chairs scraped along the wooden floor as people lined up their seats with their neighbors' so that there would be plenty of room for talking. Some people brought in notes and cups of coffee, cigarettes and soft drinks. The flourescent lights shone brightly overhead, making the room seem large and unfriendly to Rhetta.

When there were about thirty people, Rhetta decided it was time to start the meeting. Bates hadn't arrived yet. Good, she thought with malice. It'll look bad when he walks in late.

"Is everyone ready to begin?" Rhetta raised her voice above the din of conversation, and everyone began to quiet down, like chickens at bedtime. "Well, I've got some very good news for you tonight, but I

think that Sarah should be the one to tell you. Sarah?"
Rhetta looked inquiringly at her friend and Sarah rose.

"Well, the old Thompson Building is going to be
put to use." Immediately there were murmurs of surprise and questions from the townspeople. "Justus
leased it to me, and I'll be moving in soon." Sarah
smiled and her brown eyes shone with warm excitement. "Probably in about two to three weeks. Uh, it's
for my baby-apparel company. I'll need three full-time
girls and one part-time girl to sew and cut, so if any of
y'all know someone who needs a job, let me know."

A few people near Sarah patted her on the back and
whispered congratulations, but mostly the news was
met with yawns. Rhetta's heart sank.

"The next item of business is a promise that was
made last night by Mr.—" Rhetta looked up and Bates
strolled in with Nanny on his arm.

"Hello, everybody!" he shouted, and waved his
hand. He was so tall and his physical impact seemed
so abrupt and forceful that Rhetta felt compelled to
step back.

"Why, it's Bates McCabe!"

"I haven't seen him since—"

"My Lord! Hasn't he grown?"

"Handsome lookin' thing, isn't he?"

"Hey Bates! You still makin' two dates on the same
night?" This question met with a round of laughter.

Rhetta's jaw tightened. He was deliberately breaking up her meeting.

"Lord, no, Jack," Bates retorted. "I'm too old for
that foolishness. Besides, I believe Sandy must have

told the whole state of Texas about that!" Everyone laughed again. Sandy was a notorious gossip. "I couldn't get a date for years after that escapade."

Everyone laughed, that is, everyone except Rhetta. She was angry. Bates had deliberately stolen her thunder and taken control of the meeting away from her. He'd undermined her authority and made her appear foolish.

Bates looked up, as if he were just seeing Rhetta for the first time.

"Oh, I'm sorry, Rhetta! I didn't mean to interrupt your meeting. Please, excuse me." Bates led Nanny down a row at the back, shaking hands and answering murmurs of "welcome home" with a smile or a nod.

"Well, I'm sure we're all glad to see Bates has come for a *visit*. It's always nice to have city folks come by." Rhetta smiled sourly. "Now the next item of business is that Mr. Sutphen has agreed to open up his tool-manufacturing business right here in Tuckerville." This announcement was met with much more surprise and excitement than her previous announcement, and Rhetta was warmed by that fact.

"Excuse me, Miss Mayor," Bates interrupted, with affected gallantry. He rose and his presence felt like an intimidating force rushing at her. "I'd like to extend my congratulations to Steve and to Sarah. Tuckerville needs industry to keep it growing, and it's especially nice since these are some of our own people." Bates opened his mouth to say more but Rhetta rushed in.

"Thank you for your words of support Mr. Mc-Cabe, and now, I'd like to—"

"Miss Mayor? Begging your pardon, but I wasn't finished speaking, and if my memory serves me correctly, it was your daddy who always said that not letting a person from Tuckerville have his say was akin to chopping off his fingers." Bates paused.

"That's right. He's got you there!" Faye Kern bobbed her red-haired head in agreement with Bates and folded her arms across her chest.

Rhetta smiled crookedly. "Excuse me, Mr. Mc-Cabe. Please continue." Rhetta gestured with her hand.

"I'd like to make an announcement, too." Bates paused again, then walked up to the lectern, and Rhetta stepped reluctantly aside.

She felt dwarfed by his bulk, even though she knew she was tall for a woman. She also knew that he looked tall, powerful and in control. And that made her look womanly. And weak. Rhetta's temper flared.

"As you all know, I haven't just come back to visit. I've come back to live." He paused and smiled widely at the crowd. Rhetta's stomach dropped, as if in instinctive warning. "I've bought the old warehouse located east of town and I plan to manufacture computer components. It's just like manufacturing machine tools or bicycles except that it's computer parts. This isn't just a fly-by-night operation I'm planning. I've been working on a business plan for three years. Tuckerville's plant will be only the beginning. I have plans to build and operate three more plants over the next five years. Computers are not a boom business as some people think. They are, and will continue to be, an important part of a progressive society, and we can be a part of it, too.''

Bates continued speaking, but Rhetta was seething with fury and humiliation. He was reading the notes that she'd left lying on the lectern—reading her speech and changing it around. She was so angry that she wanted to rush over to him and grab the speech off the lectern and shriek, ''That's mine!'' Damn him!

''For too long now, Tuckerville has been tied to a few small businesses. I applaud the effort of Sarah and Mr. Sutphen, and I believe that all of us, together, can make a better tomorrow for Tuckerville.''

Teaming his name with two hometown favorites so that he could appear in a more favorable light, Rhetta thought bitterly.

''There's a new dream in Tuckerville, a new hope for all of us. My business has the financial support of Justus, Mr. Hopkins, our banker, and of course, my own Aunt Nanny.'' The crowd chuckled softly.

''My business will bring two hundred jobs to Tuckerville.'' The townspeople gasped, and Bates looked evenly at the audience, nodding his head in confirmation. ''That's right. Two hundred. It will be slow in starting, but I believe that if you will all work with me, we can put Tuckerville back on the map.'' Bates turned to Rhetta, and the crowd jumped to their feet and began applauding fervently.

Such news hadn't been heard in Tuckerville for thirty years. It meant increased business for every man and woman in town. But as far as Rhetta was concerned, the townspeople were like lambs going to slaughter.

"Wait a minute! Wait!" Rhetta held up her hands and stood quite still until the crowd had settled back into their seats. "Don't you remember? History is repeating itself. When the oil men from Houston came to Tuckerville promising jobs and industry and prosperity for Tuckerville, you were only too happy to accept them. But many of you went broke when the oil dried up and the jobs disappeared. This town can't take the ups and downs of a business like that or like the computer industry. I agree we need to diversify and attract new growth, but not this! Not a fledgling computer business that's more likely to go bust than not. Tuckerville needs to start with small businesses like Sarah's and help them grow gradually."

Rhetta looked pleadingly out at their stubborn faces, and when there was no response, she tried a new tactic. She flung her hands wide in a gesture of appeal. "Bates worked as a roustabout in West Texas before the oil business busted. That's when he moved into the computer industry—when he saw big money to be made. It's a growth industry just like oil was in the 1930s. Please, please, don't make the same mistake twice. We can't afford it." Rhetta put out her hands, palms upward.

"You can't afford to sit still and do nothing anymore, either," Bates retorted sharply. His eyes were an angry blue. "Would you like to comment on her statements, Justus?'' Bates still stood at the lectern and spoke quietly but forcefully.

''Yes, ahem, yes I would.'' Justus limped to the front of the hall and turned to face the crowd. ''I've known most of you all my life, just like I've known these two youngsters since they were in diapers.'' Justus gestured to Bates and Rhetta. ''And I guess I knew what was going to happen here tonight before it even happened, 'cause I kinda figured that these two would bump heads before this was all over.'' He scratched his head and looked at Rhetta and then at Bates. ''They're both smart and competitive, and that's good because that's what made America great.''

Justus stumped across the floor and several people in the crowd nodded their heads in agreement and several said, ''Amen,'' as if Justus were preaching a sermon.

''Now there's two ways to go about something like this,'' Justus continued. ''One solution is to leave them to fight it out by themselves and probably split the town into two sides. The other, is to fight it out by democratic process. What I'm saying is this, I propose that we form a Business Development Committee composed of Rhetta, Bates, Sarah and Steven Sutphen.'' He smiled wickedly and his eyes twinkled. ''And if they want to fight, they can contain their fighting to their committee meetings.''

Rhetta stole a quick glance at Bates and saw that he, too, was smiling as if in anticipation.

"Hear, hear!" Nanny shouted gleefully. The others chorused her affirmation, and Rhetta knew her coffin was sealed.

If he wouldn't look at me that way, I could hate him. This will never work. He's a wanderer. Rhetta's shoulders sagged, and she glanced at Bates.

She'd be on that darned committee, but she wouldn't like it one bit. He smiled gently at her, a conciliatory smile. Well, she wasn't going to smile about it, anyway.

Rhetta could hear the muffled voices of Nanny and Bates from the parlor inside the house. She knew they were talking about her.

The stars were out in full force tonight. Thousands of them dotted the sky, like glitter thrown on a black ceiling. There was no breeze to speak of, just an occasional puff now and then.

The door creaked when Bates opened it and stepped onto the front porch. Rhetta looked away from him and sat in her usual position on the porch railing.

"I want to talk to you," Bates said quietly.

Rhetta kept her head averted.

"Nanny wrote me a letter because she was worried about you. She wanted to help, so she wrote to me, asking me to come down here and at least consider Tuckerville as a possible site for my manufacturing plant. I wouldn't have considered it, if it hadn't been for that letter she wrote me." Bates paused with his hands on his hips and wondered what Rhetta was thinking. "I grew up here, too, Rhetta."

"But you left." Her voice was barely audible and she kept her face averted.

Bates let out a sigh. "Of course I left. I was nineteen and wild. At that point I needed something more than Tuckerville had to offer." Bates grinned self-deprecatingly and looked out at the sleepy lights of the houses on their street and wondered if he could ever make her understand.

"And now you don't?" she asked sarcastically. She looked at him, something she'd promised herself she wouldn't do—because when she looked at him, she didn't want to fight him. Didn't want to fight for Tuckerville. She wanted to melt against him and feel his warm, strong arms around her.

She'd never dreamed she could feel that way about him again, that adolescent breathlessness, especially not now that she had decided she didn't really like him. But then she realized that it wasn't that she didn't like him personally; she just didn't like him trying to involve the town in a risky business.

"No, I don't," he said quietly. "I think everything I want is right here in Tuckerville."

Rhetta didn't look at him when he said that, but her heart started thumping against her ribs.

"You'll get tired of Tuckerville and want to leave, just like you did when you were nineteen," Rhetta stated confidently.

"Why don't you trust me, Rhetta?" A puzzled light was in his eyes. His cheekbones were highlighted by the soft moon's glow.

"Because I don't. Look at your history. While I stayed in Tuckerville and worked, you were eating high off the hog in the big city, playing around, exploring new things, leaving whenever the mood struck you—"

"You really resent that, don't you? But you shouldn't. It was your choice."

"I couldn't leave," she shot back. "I'd made a promise, and I don't go back on my promises." Rhetta turned away from him and gazed out at the night. The stars were winking here and there, and the pearly moon was bigger than it was last night. She wished Bates had returned under different circumstances.

"Rhetta," Bates said, moving closer to her, "I'm not going to be punished because I didn't stay here. What I learned out there can help Tuckerville."

"It can also hurt Tuckerville, Bates." Rhetta's tone was earnest, and her eyes met his directly. "Tuckerville doesn't have any major businesses, just mom-and-pop shops. If you open the plant here and hire two hundred people, if your business even makes it through the first year—"

"It will," he interrupted her confidently.

"If it does," she continued, "then sometime over the next ten years you'll hit hard times and people will get laid off. You'll leave Tuckerville worse off than it was before. The long-term impact of your business could kill Tuckerville." Rhetta slid off the porch railing and crossed her arms in front of her. Her dress swirled softly around her knees as she turned to face him.

"Rhetta, the last thing in the world I'd want to do is hurt Tuckerville or you."

Rhetta's heart leaped in her chest, and she cursed her susceptibility to him.

"This isn't just some idea I dreamed up last week, Rhetta. I've been working for over three years on this, planning, making contacts—everything. You seem to think I'm a playboy who just wants to take a ride on the town. It's not like that, Rhetta. *I'm* not like that. My business *will* succeed."

Rhetta sighed and shrugged. "I hope so, Bates. I really hope so."

It was no use arguing about it. She'd just have to save Tuckerville as best she could when the time came. Because Rhetta had no doubt in her mind that the time would come when his business would flounder.

She turned and walked into the house, resigned to accepting Bates's business but unhappy about what the future held for Tuckerville. And, oddly enough, for Bates.

Rhetta pulled the crisp white sheet up to her chin, turned her pillow over to the cool side and stared up at the ceiling. She could hear the oak branches scraping against the side of the house each time the wind blew.

It wasn't fair that she should be so attracted to a man whom she was certain would be gone in less than a year. It wasn't fair that he should have hair so black and curly that it made her want to wrap a curl around her finger and then kiss his neck. Nor that his skin should be so dark and tight across his cheekbones. He had an effortless beauty. It was evident that he rarely looked in a mirror except to shave and that he was more comfortable in jeans and boots than in a suit and tie. But his power didn't come from a navy-blue three-piece suit—it came from the force of his character. He was a natural leader. A born leader.

He had the clean, fluid lines of a long-distance runner, but Rhetta doubted he ran regularly to maintain his lean, hard-muscled physique. That he was blessed with eyes the color of bluebonnets and straight white teeth against his rugged tan did not alter how Rhetta felt about him. But it did alter how her body responded to him.

During the past two days, Rhetta had cursed her body a million times for the uncontrollable heat that seeped through her limbs whenever he was near. He didn't even have to be in the same room with her and her heart would accelerate of its own accord just at the thought that he was nearby.

No, no, no! she scolded herself fervently. *I can't think that way!* He'll be gone in less than a year and some other woman in another town will dream about him. *But not me,* she pledged silently, and was frightened by the lack of conviction her vow held.

Chapter Four

"Where do you want to put Susie?" Rhetta asked, gesturing to the one-armed female mannequin. They had tied rags over Susie's chest and hips so that she would be modestly dressed when Bates and Steven Sutphen arrived to help clean Sarah's shop.

"Put her up front on the sidewalk. Everyone will get a kick when they see her dressed up in rags like that." Sarah grinned, and even though there was dirt streaked across Sarah's cheek, Rhetta thought her friend had a quiet kind of beauty that had aged well.

Rhetta lugged the mannequin outside and placed her on the sidewalk, lifting Susie's one arm up, as if in greeting. She paused to rest a moment and to enjoy the slight breeze. Raising her hand to shield her eyes, she looked up. The sun was not quite straight overhead, but it felt as if it were. Rhetta pulled her blouse away from her back and felt the sweat trickle down her spine. She walked back inside the airless building and went to the back of the shop to begin sweeping.

"Looks like the rest of the Business Development Committee decided not to come," Rhetta said, noting the absence of Bates and Steven.

"Now you know Bates said he had a meeting with the bankers this morning, and as for Steven, I—"

"And as for Steven, what?" Steven Sutphen walked in and took off his baseball hat, his gray eyes lighting up as he looked at Sarah.

Sarah's hand fluttered up as if to smooth her hair into place and then back down to her side again.

"Hello, Sarah," Steven said quietly.

Sarah bobbed her head in greeting and looked nervously around for Rhetta. Rhetta smothered a smile at Sarah's sudden shyness and stopped sweeping.

"Hi there. We sure are glad you came along. Sarah and I were just wondering how we were going to lift those heavy sewing machines after we get this place cleaned up." Rhetta smiled at Steven, and he seemed to be thankful that she had stepped in to ease Sarah's discomfort.

"Well, when Bates gets here, we can take my truck up to Sarah's house, pack up the machines and then haul them down here."

"Thank you, Steven. That'd be real nice of you." Sarah twisted her fingers into the rag she'd been using to wipe down the windowsills, and she faltered under Steven's steady gaze.

There was such a yearning look in Steven's gray eyes and such a frightened, doelike look in Sarah's brown eyes that Rhetta wanted to walk over and say, "Look you two, it's obvious that you'd both like to be with one another, so why don't you just quit hemming and hawing and get on with it. The way you two are courting, you'll both be ninety before you have your first date!" But she couldn't do that. She had to be more tactful, more diplomatic.

"Tell you what, Steven," Rhetta said easily, "if you could help Sarah drag those boxes of trash out front and down to that dumpster on the corner, then Faye Kern won't come yell at us about slowing up the traffic going to her café." They both laughed at her prediction of Faye's behavior. "And speaking of Faye, I don't know about Sarah, but I'd love a sandwich."

"Yes, that sounds good," Sarah agreed, and looked around the shop to appraise their progress.

"Well, why don't you two go on over there and just bring a BLT back for me, okay?" Rhetta asked. She met Sarah's panicked brown eyes with firm reassurance, and when Sarah looked pleadingly at her, Rhetta hardened her heart.

"Sounds fine to me," Steven said a little too casually.

"Oh, Rhetta. Why don't you come with us. It's so hot in here, and we both need a break."

"No, I'm going to have to leave early, so I want to get my hours in now. Go on. I don't want to hear another word." Rhetta put her hand up to stop any protest Sarah might utter.

Steven grinned and Sarah smiled weakly. Rhetta turned her back and began sweeping again. She heard their footsteps reach the door, a nervous little cough from Sarah as Steven waited for her to precede him and then the clomp of Steven's boots as they reached the pavement.

Rhetta turned with a satisfied smile and began sweeping out the dust and dirt. The floor was black-and-white-checked tile and was yellowed in the corners from wax buildup and age but still functional. The green walls would need to be washed, patched and painted, but that would be a relatively easy task.

She had filled the dustpan twice before she'd progressed halfway across the room. The front half of the room wasn't nearly as dirty as the back half, though, and it went much faster after that. Rhetta worked efficiently, humming an old folk song to keep her rhythm steady.

When she'd swept the entire floor, Rhetta didn't pause to sit down and rest. She was afraid that if she stopped, she'd drop from sheer fatigue.

Instead, she slowly pulled an old metal pail from a hook in the bathroom and filled it with hot, soapy suds. She started scrubbing at the back of the room and worked her way forward, squirting the dirty suds off with a garden hose and then sweeping the water out as she went.

"Don't tell me." Bates paused in the doorway, looked at Rhetta down on her hands and knees, and held up a hand as if to ward off any comments. "You're Cinderella, waiting for Prince Charming. Well, you don't have to wait any longer, darling. I'm here."

He grinned down at her, and if Rhetta hadn't been so hot and tired, she would have made a snappy rejoinder. As it was, she could only smile weakly. She stopped scrubbing and looked at his attire.

"You wore *that* to the bank meeting?" Rhetta's gaze skimmed over his faded straight-legged blue jeans and his old, pale blue work shirt, which was rolled up at the sleeves. Even in his grubbies he looked good, Rhetta thought. Very good.

"What's the matter with this? These are my very best tennis shoes." Bates smiled that half-grin of his that always made her gaze skitter away and her heart knock against her ribs like a car engine running on cheap gasoline. "No, I didn't wear these clothes. I went home to change before coming here. I told you I'd be a little late." Bates pulled an oatmeal cookie out of the paper sack he was carrying. "Want a cookie?" he offered.

"I didn't think you'd come at all." Rhetta took the cookie from him by way of answering. She knew Nanny had made these cookies for him late last night. Nanny spoiled him shamelessly.

"Why not?"

"I don't know. I just didn't." *Because men like you don't have the tenacity to stick with anything. Not one job, not one town and not one woman.*

"What do you want me to do?" Bates asked.

"Well. First I want another cookie." Rhetta smiled impishly up at him. He handed her another cookie. Rhetta looked around the room. "Why don't you go along behind me as I scrub and rinse off the dirty suds with the hose and then sweep the dirty water out the front."

He nodded and reached for the hose and broom.

"You really do look a little like Cinderella." Bates's mouth quirked upward as he squirted an area of dirty soap.

"Well, you certainly don't look like Prince Charming," Rhetta said dryly.

"What about now?" He smiled widely and raised his eyebrows like an old-fashioned movie star. Rhetta sat back, placed her arms behind her to support her body and considered him.

"No." She shook her head. "Now you look like Dudley Do-Right."

"I'll save you Nell!" Bates cried in a fair imitation of the cartoon character, nimbly knelt beside her on the floor and slid one arm under her legs and the other behind her back. He feigned a straining attempt to lift her. "Hmmm. I can't seem to pick you up," he said teasingly, his face inches from hers. His eyes were dancing with flirtatious amusement. "It's funny how that happens, isn't it?" he asked, letting his lips trail along her jawbone and nipping sensuously at her earlobe.

Rhetta swallowed, wanting nothing more than to stay in his arms but also wanting to get away from this man who'd had a reputation since high school as a womanizer.

"It's funny how you maneuver to insult me," she said nervously, moving her head to avoid a kiss. Rhetta spied the garden hose lying harmlessly beside him. She leaned back fully, as if to assuage his growing hunger, and then deftly snatched the hose and squirted him full in the face.

Bates shut his eyes as the full force of the cold water hit him. Rhetta dropped the hose, scrambled out from beneath him and retreated to the back of the shop. Bates grabbed the hose and stood up.

"Bates, I'm sorry, I swear," she said, giggling breathlessly.

He advanced toward her slowly, a smile tugging at the corner of his mouth. Rhetta raised her hand to block the water. "Bates, please. I swear I'll never do it again. I swear. I—" Rhetta shut her mouth quickly, then gasped as the cold water hit her. She turned her head and tried to block the stream with her hands. She could sense Bates coming closer to her and she took short steps out of the corner and then made a run for the bucket of soapy water.

Bates turned and pursued her. They were inches apart when Rhetta dumped the bucket over him. No longer afraid of the water since she was already wet, she grabbed for the hose and crimped it so that only a trickle came out. Rhetta's breath was coming in short gasps, and her eyes were shining with childish delight. Bates laughed and grabbed her wrist.

"Ow, stop it. That hurts!" Rhetta feigned pain in her wrist, and he quickly released her. She grabbed the hose from him and started squirting him, drenching him as thoroughly as he'd drenched her.

"Argh!" Bates lunged for her, and Rhetta stumbled backwards out of his reach, still in control of the hose. He finally grabbed her waist, as if to tackle her, and Rhetta fell against him as they continued to laugh. He sank down to the floor, carrying her with him.

Her white T-shirt was drenched and clinging to her and her shorts were soaked and dirty from her sitting on the floor, scrubbing. Their faces were but inches apart, Rhetta lying across him, his breath fanning her cheeks as they slowly regained regular breathing.

Their eyes remained locked, sexual tension binding them and then building between them. And it was Rhetta who made the first move this time.

She leaned down ever so slowly and touched her lips to his. They were surprisingly soft. Coherent thought fled as Rhetta was engulfed by sensation. All she was aware of was the warmth of his hot lips, nibbling hungrily at hers, the raspy feeling of his callused hands which slid up her slick skin as if her body were lightly oiled. He pulled at her bottom lip with his teeth, gently sucking until Rhetta could stand no more.

She traced a line of kisses down the column of his throat until her lips paused at the base of his neck. She watched in fascination as his pulse quickened. She wondered how many other women had made his heart beat that quickly, and rolled away as she guessed the answer was probably more than she cared to know.

"Rhetta?" Bates circled her wrists with his hands.

"Sorry. I . . . I guess I got a little carried away." Rhetta stood up quickly and began squeezing the excess water out of the tail of her T-shirt.

"What's the matter?"

"Nothing. I just forgot something." Rhetta bent and picked up the scrub brush she had discarded earlier.

"Rhetta, you can't just turn away from me like that."

"I'm sure there are hundreds of other women who'd be willing to . . ." Rhetta sat back on her heels and left the rest unsaid.

"That's not the point and you damned well know it," Bates said tersely.

"I don't have to answer to you for my actions or lack of them. Maybe I don't want to be left holding the bag when your company goes bankrupt and you leave town." Rhetta bent and scrubbed the floor vigorously.

"Rhetta—" Bates's lips thinned, but instead of pursuing the argument, he began sweeping out the dirty water. His features were pulled into brooding, thoughtful lines, which only added to his dangerous appearance.

His self-control surprised Rhetta. She had expected Bates to use his considerable seductive powers to woo her back into complacency or for him to react like a spoiled three-year-old. But he didn't use either of those tactics.

He turned his thoughts inward, revealing only a furrowed brow and intense concentration. Perhaps there was a little more depth to him than Rhetta had realized.

"Hello, you two!" Sarah called out gaily as she and Steven entered the shop. Sarah's gaze ran over Rhetta's and Bates's wet clothes, but Sarah had seen Bates's set face and Rhetta's thin-lipped regard, so thankfully, Sarah said nothing about their wet appearance.

"Hello," Rhetta greeted them, and stood up.

"Here's your sandwich, Rhetta." Sarah handed her the sandwich and turned to Bates. "Bates, I'm sorry I didn't even think to bring you anything, but it would just take me a minute if you'd—"

"No thanks, Sarah. I had a bite to eat before I left home." His face was still grim, but his eyes crinkled in a semblance of appreciation at Sarah's offer.

Sarah took Rhetta's place on the floor, scrubbing, while Steven swept as Bates hosed down the floor. Rhetta sat down on a windowsill and munched her sandwich hurriedly. The afternoon heat was turning the humid, unairconditioned room into a sweat bath. Her clothes were sticking to her again as she polished off the sandwich.

"Rhetta, you look so hot. Why don't you go outside and clean the plate-glass window?" Sarah suggested. "There's a slight breeze out there."

"That sounds good," Rhetta agreed. She picked up a rag and some window cleaner in a squirt bottle and went outside.

"Bates, I can hose this floor down and sweep, too. I believe it'll be a whole lot easier if you could clean the inside of the window while Rhetta's cleaning the outside," Steven suggested.

"Fine," Bates said shortly. Fine, hell, he thought. Now I'll have to look directly at her. Bates picked up a clean rag and another bottle of spray cleaner and advanced to the window. Rhetta's murky form was just visible through the dirty glass.

Rhetta stretched up her arm to the top of the window and then wiped down in a circular motion. She turned her cloth to the clean side.

Bates squirted the window with the cleaner and reached up just above his head and wiped straight down, making a clear spot so that he could see Rhetta, separated from him by only a few inches.

Rhetta and Bates squirted the cleaner at the same time, and Rhetta glared in irritation at his strong-featured face, even though he wasn't looking at her, but wiping vigorously at the streaks on the window. She peered through the clear glass at him, willing herself to be unconscious of him as they washed off the dirt with simultaneous strokes.

Bates seemed so comfortable with his body and his sexuality that it was almost unnatural, Rhetta thought, then realized her idea was clearly a contradiction in terms.

As she continued cleaning the window, she remembered how he was completely unaware of the way his muscles rippled when he stretched, and at night, when he leaned back in the rocker in the parlor watching TV,

how his thigh muscles flexed and then relaxed with
each motion of the rocker. He's just like an animal,
yawning and stretching all the time, she thought with
civilized distaste. He really was disgusting. Disgusting.

Rhetta rolled her eyes as she felt the tingly sensation begin to build at her sensual thoughts. The plain
truth was that she found him very sexually attractive.
But the thought was still too much for her to admit.

Bates surreptitiously watched as Rhetta scrubbed,
with her arm high above her head, causing her still-
damp T-shirt to pull even tighter against her breasts.
She lost her balance momentarily, and her breasts were
crushed against the pane directly in front of Bates's
eyes. Bates bit hard on the inside of his cheek and then
sank to his knees to rub angrily at a speck on the glass.

Damn. Why did she have to be such a goody two
shoes and have such an incredibly sensual body? It
was, well, lush, he thought and laughed shortly at the
word that had popped into his brain.

Rhetta looked up at him sharply through the window when he laughed, but Bates didn't meet her blue-
eyed gaze. He knew she would see the desire written in
his eyes if he so much as glanced at her, so he kept his
attention studiously fixed on the glass.

He wondered suddenly if she were a virgin and then
dismissed the thought. No one could reach the age of
twenty-eight and still be a virgin. Especially not with
all that closely harnessed heat she had stored up in her.
Why, just one look at her that first day he'd seen her
had been enough to practically set him on fire.

But it was her flat, pale blue stare that kept him at a distance. It wasn't icy or cold or hard, just straight and unwavering. She didn't demand respect, she commanded it. She was, he conceded, quite a lady.

Rhetta had always thought that July was the hottest month of the summer, even though everyone else always said that August was. Maybe it was because in July she knew she still had to wade through August and September before cooler weather came along.

Moving along at a leisurely pace, she pulled a flower from a crape myrtle bush as she walked by Mrs. Bookerton's house and smiled faintly as the sound of Minnie's loving scolding of her dog, Sir Francis Drake, floated from the house. The sun was just setting and the locusts had started humming in the trees. She skirted baby Lauren's tricycle, which was turned upside down in the middle of the sidewalk. The older children had obviously been playing hopscotch and Rhetta stepped around that too, stripping a leaf from the stem of the flower she held and letting it fall to the ground. Rhetta turned the corner and, seeing Bates's shiny black car parked in front of Sarah's, warned her heart not to race.

He'd been out of town a lot lately. He'd gone to Houston to move his belongings to Tuckerville and then had returned to Houston again to secure contracts for his product. He'd been away so often that she'd hardly seen him at all since they'd moved Sarah into her shop.

But now Bates's car was in front of Sarah's house; he'd come back for the first Business Development Committee meeting. Somehow, she'd known he'd be there even though he hadn't shown up at the boarding house for dinner.

That's why she'd selected the pale blue dress she was wearing. It had cap sleeves and a rounded neck with tiny scallops, pearl buttons down the front and a full skirt that swirled down around her knees. Rhetta felt pretty in it but not provocative.

She walked up the pathway lined with pink begonias to Sarah's door and let herself in. "Hello. I'm here," she called out.

"Hello." Sarah's brown eyes were lit up like two candles, and Rhetta knew, right then and there, that Sarah and Steven had been seeing each other quite a bit.

Rhetta walked into the small dining room, noting the rich aroma of freshly brewed coffee. Bates and Steven were seated at a small round table, with china blue mugs of the hot liquid in their hands.

"Hi, Rhetta," Steven said, taking a sip of his coffee. Bates leaned back in his chair, and Rhetta could feel his gaze roving over her curves. She quickly pulled out a chair and sat down, attempting to hide part of her body from him.

"Why don't you sit down," Bates offered, mocking her hurried effort to divert his attention.

Rhetta didn't acknowledge his remark; instead she busied herself with pulling a small pocket notebook from her purse.

"Rhetta, would you like some coffee?" Sarah stood at the counter that separated the pale yellow kitchen from the dining room.

"Yes, please, Sarah. That would be nice." Rhetta scooted her chair up closer to the table and avoided Bates's gaze. Why in the world does he stare at me like that? It's irritating, she thought.

"There you go." Sarah set Rhetta's coffee down in front of her and then seated herself beside Steven. Steven placed his arm around the back of Sarah's chair.

"Well," Rhetta said. "I guess the first item of business is—"

"To elect a chairman," Bates said in a challenging voice. Rhetta's mouth opened and then shut. She'd assumed that since she was mayor, she'd be the chairman.

"All right," Rhetta said tightly. "Since there are only four of us, let's just write down who we want on a sheet of paper, and then Sarah can tally the votes," Rhetta said confidently. "Is that agreeable?" She looked pointedly at Bates. He'll probably throw a fit when I win, she thought.

"Fine with me," Bates agreed easily, and Steven nodded his head in agreement.

"All right. Everyone write down who you want as chairman of this committee." Rhetta picked up her pen and wrote in bold letters, *Rhetta Tucker*, folded the slip in two and passed it to Sarah.

When everyone had passed their votes over, Sarah shuffled them and then unfolded the first one. "One vote for Bates McCabe," she announced.

Bates grinned and Rhetta smirked, knowing Bates had voted for himself.

"One vote for Rhetta Tucker."

Rhetta smiled confidently.

"Another vote for Bates and...another vote for Bates. That's three votes to one. Bates is the chairman." Sarah didn't meet Rhetta's eyes.

Rhetta couldn't believe it. How could Sarah turn on her like that? Did she honestly want an unscrupulous man like Bates running their town?

"Now," Bates said, his voice full of authority and purpose, "I'll need a secretary. Will anyone volunteer for the job or shall I appoint someone?"

His secretary! Why she'd rather die than be humiliated by being his underling. It would be all over town tomorrow that Bates had taken over and Rhetta was his mousy little secretary.

"I think," Sarah interjected hurriedly, "that since it's customary in most towns for the mayor to sit on the committee but not chair it, it's probably also customary for the mayor not to be secretary." Sarah attempted to explain her vote for Bates and to salve Rhetta's hurt feelings. "And knowing how poorly Steven writes—" Sarah smiled shyly at Steven "—I think it would be in everyone's best interest for me to be secretary." She smiled at them, and Rhetta smiled back genuinely.

It wasn't that Rhetta was being childish; it just seemed to her that nobody saw through Bates the way she did. And she was irritated that they kept giving him more and more power over Tuckerville's future.

"This meeting is now called to order." Bates slammed his fist on the table and Rhetta jumped. "How am I doing so far, mayor?" Bates grinned at Rhetta as she looked askance at him.

"Fine. But don't bang on the table. We don't use gavels in Tuckerville."

"Yeah, I suppose you're right," he agreed. "In Tuckerville, too many people would die of heart failure if I banged like that." Bates chuckled and an unwilling smile pulled at Rhetta's lips.

"The first order of business is to discuss town improvements," Bates stated decisively.

This certainly won't be a democratic committee with him leading it, Rhetta thought.

"Any suggestions?" Bates asked.

"Yes." Rhetta folded her hands on top of the table and sat forward. "That cracked fountain in front of the courthouse looks awful. How do we expect people to want to stay in Tuckerville if it looks so run-down and homely?"

Sarah nodded her head in agreement.

"Excuse me," Bates cut in smoothly. "I was speaking of town *business* improvements. This isn't a beauty-contest committee," he added derisively.

Steven chuckled and picked up his coffee to take a sip. "What about trying to contact that air-brakes-manufacturing company that's been scouting this area for a site to build their plant?" Steven offered.

"That sounds interesting," Bates said, thoughtfully rubbing his knuckles across his chin.

"Are you crazy?" Rhetta asked, and looked at both men seated across from her with wide eyes. "Tuckerville has all the new business it can support right now. What we need to do is improve and nurture what we already have before we haul off and invite *more* trouble into town," she said scathingly.

"I agree with Rhetta," Sarah said slowly. "I think Tuckerville has more than it can handle right now. If a town tries to grow too quickly, it won't be equipped to support the commerce it has—environmentally, economically or socially. We have many existing businesses that could be built up and improved. It doesn't make sense to bring in new ones and forget about the ones we've already got."

Rhetta nodded and felt more confident now that Sarah had agreed with her.

"It's the law of survival," Bates said, and shrugged his broad shoulders. "The weak get winnowed out and the stronger, better businesses stay around to grow."

"That's a good way of putting it, Bates," Steven added. "Why not put our efforts and money into attracting new technological businesses that will complement your company—" he nodded to Bates "—and make Tuckerville a mecca for technological manufacturing, like Silicon Valley in California is a mecca for computer wizards."

"Exactly," Bates said.

"Now just hold on a minute you two." Rhetta raised her hand. "I'd say our first priority is to make sure Sarah's and both of your manufacturing plants are operating well for two years before we try to bring in more businesses. The town simply cannot support an avalanche of industry. It isn't a matter of attracting businesses anymore. They'll come. It's a matter of developing the businesses that are already on the drawing board," Rhetta stated emphatically.

"I don't know about Steven, but I really don't want or need a committee sticking their nose into my business to tell me how to run it," Bates said with a warning note in his voice.

"That's right," Steven said. "No man wants somebody stepping in to run a company which he started from scratch. If that's the function of this committee, we'll run more businesses off than we'll attract."

"I'm not talking about running your business," Rhetta argued, scarcely able to keep her voice down. "I'm talking about community development." Rhetta folded her arms across her chest in a huff, and Bates's eyes narrowed.

"I think what Rhetta is saying," Sarah intervened tactfully, "is the function of the committee is to act as a support group, not as a chamber of commerce."

"Support group?" Bates laughed scornfully. "My God, Sarah, this isn't a divorce-counseling center. We're talking about developing businesses for the community, not about any of this ridiculous psychology."

"She means like a business club," Rhetta said hotly. "Supporting each other as—"

"This is a committee, Rhetta, not a club." Bates sliced his hand through the air, and his black brows rushed together in a formidable line. "The name of this committee is Business Development," he said, punctuating his words by tapping his finger on the table, "and that's what we're going to do." Bates sat back in his chair and glared at Rhetta.

"Aren't we going to take a vote on this, *Mister* Chairman?" Rhetta asked tartly.

"Why not?" Bates answered silkily. "All those in favor of improving the existing businesses in Tuckerville, raise your hand." He looked at Rhetta expectantly.

Rhetta and Sarah both raised their hands. Rhetta's light blue eyes locked with the fiery dark blue of Bates's, and her heart began to pound.

"And all those in favor of attracting other technological businesses to Tuckerville, raise your hands." Bates and Steven raised their hands briefly. "All right, it's a tie. Since I'm chairman, I'll cast the deciding vote in favor of attracting technological businesses. The vote is three to two."

"Excuse me, Mr. Chairman," Sarah said quietly, "but I believe you voted twice. The chairman cannot vote unless there is a tie. The vote was two to one in favor of improving existing businesses."

A look of grudging respect crossed Bates's features as he eyed Sarah, and Rhetta was surprised to feel a twinge of jealousy. She wished that he admired her, too.

"I stand corrected." Bates grinned. "At the next meeting we'll discuss what our first project will be."

He looked at Rhetta, and a little chill shimmied up her spine; she felt he wasn't quite conceding victory. "This meeting is adjourned."

Rhetta scooted her chair out from the table and stood up, immediately feeling Bates's gaze run over her figure and then come to rest on her face. She avoided his gaze scrupulously. "I've got to run, Sarah. Thanks for the coffee."

Bates stood. "I've got to run, too."

Rhetta hurried to the door and immediately pulled it open and scurried down the steps, knowing that Bates was not far behind. She peeked back over her shoulder. Bates's frame filled the doorway, blocking out the yellow light from the house until Sarah flicked the porch light on, illuminating Bates, making him appear a larger-than-life figure on the porch.

"Bye, y'all," Rhetta called out, and waved at Sarah and Steven. The couple were standing on the front porch, holding hands as Bates descended the steps.

"Hey," Bates called as he watched the pale blue of her dress floating down the street. "Hey, Rhetta. Do you want a ride back?"

Rhetta took a deep breath and kept walking. If she got into that car with him, she knew what would happen because she'd been dreaming about it happening for the past two weeks. She could and she would avoid temptation. Bates McCabe was not going to leave with her heart when his business failed in a year.

Chapter Five

"Why they always have the church picnic in late August every year, I'm sure I don't know," Nanny said with exasperation to no one in particular as she poured a glass of lemonade for herself and wiped her brow with her lace-edged handkerchief. "Surely is hot today," Nanny added as she looked out at the vigorous volleyball game going on between two groups of teenagers.

"It surely is," Rhetta agreed. She scooped a round ball of homemade peach ice cream into a bowl for one of the younger children waiting at the refreshment table. "Here you go, darlin'." She handed the bowl of ice cream to the blond-haired little girl, whose chin barely reached the table.

The little girl darted off to sit under a tree by the water with a group of her friends. Rhetta smiled after the little girl and reached up to curl an auburn strand of hair behind her ear as her gaze traveled to where Justus and Bates were playing horseshoes in the shade of a small cluster of pine trees.

"Well, I guess that's about all of them for a while," Nanny said tiredly, indicating the children.

"I believe so, Nanny. You go on and sit with Minnie for a while. You've been on your feet all day. These church picnics get more tiring every year." Rhetta wiped some crumbs off the red plastic tablecloth and shooed a fly away from the sandwiches, which were covered by a damp tea towel to keep them fresh.

"I believe I will sit down for a spell," Nanny agreed. "That volleyball group ought to be coming in pretty soon, and they're likely to be thirsty and hungry. I'll come back over when I see them returning." Nanny picked up a plastic cup of lemonade and walked slowly over to a group of chairs beneath an awning where they'd sing hymns tonight and roast marshmallows.

Rhetta busied herself with straightening up the table and looked over at Bates again. He was in top physical shape now from all the construction connected with opening his computer plant. He looked as strong and hard as an oil field worker. His well-muscled forearms were exposed beneath his blue cotton shirt, and his long legs were turning an even darker shade of brown in the afternoon sunshine.

He'd been the local hero all summer long. Tuckerville was filled with a devouring interest in his comings and goings. He'd been on the front page of the weekly newspaper more often than the President. Whenever he sat down at the boarding-house dinner table, everyone got all excited and solicitous. You'd think he was Clark Gable come back from the dead, Rhetta thought wryly.

This afternoon he'd gone out swimming in the lake with some of the teenagers and had come back with a trail of three moon-eyed teenage girls, who'd hung on his arms until he began playing a lengthy game of horseshoes with Justus. The girls had wandered off eventually to join in a volleyball game after failing to attract Bates's attention.

Rhetta had been standing at the refreshment table, just the way she was now, and Bates had walked over. The black curls in his hair had been damp from his swim and his madras swimming trunks were just drying when he approached. He'd looked quietly at her, and Rhetta had met his fiery blue eyes with all the coolness she could muster.

"Why don't you come for a swim with me?" he'd asked softly, noting her black swimsuit straps peeking from beneath the pale pink cotton sundress she was wearing.

There'd been a challenging glint in his blue eyes that got harder and harder for Rhetta to resist. But Rhetta hadn't even been able to answer. She'd just shaken her head no.

Every time she came near him their eyes locked in a way that made talking impossible. They both knew what it was between them. Words were useless in the sexual tension that made Rhetta aware of the way his black hair curled invitingly over his collar, the way his white teeth were slowly revealed when he parted his lips in a roguish smile, as if he knew she wanted him and yet was denying herself the satisfaction that only he could bring. She would watch as his glance moved over her lips, which always parted invitingly, and then back up to her eyes, which Rhetta hoped revealed nothing of her feelings for him.

She knew that she desired him with a white-hot passion that had not diminished during the summer, as she had told herself it would. Instead, it had intensified until Rhetta had thought she might spontaneously burst into flames whenever he was near her. He seemed to fill every place he occupied until there was no oxygen left for Rhetta to breathe.

Perhaps if she were different and could just have sex with him and then walk away without a thought, all of the tension would leave her body in one big flood of release. But even as she thought that, Rhetta knew she couldn't do it. She wasn't made that way.

She'd dream up little fantasies and imagine them getting married and having children and Bates being the nice, steady man that she knew he wasn't.

Perhaps that was why he set off such a wild longing in her; because he was untamed. His mere presence was enough to start a pleasant buzzing among the women, whether they were eight or eighty.

Even Sarah, so in love with Steven right now, would flush a little and stammer when Bates would tease her flirtatiously. It took just one cocked eyebrow or his devastating half-smile, which had flipped more than one heart, to make Rhetta realize that Bates McCabe was not, would never be, the kind of man she'd be happily married to. And for Rhetta, there simply wasn't any other way she'd get involved with him sexually.

He had surprised her by his hard, dedicated work, both on his manufacturing plant, which had been running for about one week now, and on the Business Development Committee. It had surprised her because she'd guessed that he'd tire of the work before his business ever opened, like a child who begs for a new toy and then tires of it after a few minutes.

Rhetta pulled her thoughts back to the present as she watched Justus, Bates, and a few other volleyball players who had tired of the game approach the table. Bates's shirt was open at the collar, exposing the black hair on his chest. His shirt fit snugly enough across his chest that she could see the form of his muscular chest and shoulders easily.

"Well, Rhetta," Justus said as he stumped across the lawn toward her, "I guess it's just about that time."

"Time for what?" Rhetta asked, busily filling cups with ice and lemonade, schooling her gaze to look at anything but Bates. "Another lemonade?" she suggested. "You look like you need some."

"I could do with a drink." Justus took the paper cup she extended to him and leaned heavily on the table. "No, it's about time for the first heat of the rowboat races. You know, for all the single adults."

"Oh," Rhetta said, with mild interest. "Who's my partner?"

"Well, let's see, I can't quite recall. Was it Joey Heckenkemper, Bates?" Justus removed his hat and scratched his head.

"Oh, I hope not, I was his partner last year," Rhetta said. "We came in last place."

Bates finished his lemonade and wiped his mouth with the back of his hand. "I'm your partner."

Rhetta could feel the weight of his stare as he watched her and waited for her to react to his statement. But Rhetta didn't.

"The first heat is going out now. There are five rowboats and nine teams, so we'll participate in the second heat. I'll come get you when it's time to go," Bates said.

Rhetta turned and poured more lemonade into the cups and handed some to the people lining up at the refreshment table. Only then did she turn to meet Bates's intent gaze.

"All right," she said softly. And to herself, she added, with mild irritation, *why do they have to call them heats, anyway? And I'm not going to take off my shift and just wear my swimming suit like I normally would, either. No way,* she thought. It would be inviting trouble.

Bates moved off to talk to some of the people in the crowd that had gathered and Rhetta continued pouring the lemonade. Justus still stood by the table and watched her. She met his gaze coolly, knowingly; Justus Burns had drawn the names for the rowboat races.

Justus coughed a little, looked up at the sun and then moved away.

"Rhetta! Come on," Bates called from where he was talking to the single adults who had just come back from the first heat. Rhetta waved back at him and wiped her sticky hands on a wet dishrag to remove the lemonade.

"Nanny? Can you handle this all by yourself?" Rhetta asked, knowing what the answer would be before she even asked.

"Lord, yes. Run on, Rhetta, you're holding up the entire race," Nanny admonished.

"All right," Rhetta said as she walked away. She steeled herself when she saw Bates had removed his shirt. This was going to be a difficult race.

When she reached the group where Bates stood talking, he grabbed her hand playfully and boasted, "We're going to take first place." Then, sliding a quick glance at Rhetta, he added, "Rhetta's rowing. I'm directing." The crowd chuckled good-naturedly.

Rhetta smiled slightly at his teasing, and her heart lightened as he kept hold of her hand and pulled her down to the line of boats on the bank of the lake.

The sun was very low in the sky, and the breeze was a bit cooler. The sky had colored a rosy-violet against the brilliant yellow-white of the setting sun. Most of the teams had already chosen their rowboats. There were two left: a shiny red one and a forest-green one that had seen better days. Rhetta chose the red one.

"Why the red one?" Bates asked casually.

"Because the green one doesn't look like it will make it across the lake and back, let alone win the race." Rhetta slipped off her sandals, helped Bates to push the boat into the water and then quickly stepped in.

She waved at Sarah and Steven. They had participated in the first heat and were now standing on the shore, holding hands. Sarah's face was a study in contentment; Steven looked proud and happy. Love really did change people.

Rhetta looked over at Justus, who was preparing to start them off. He raised his hand as a signal to get ready.

"On your marks, get set, go!" Justus shouted.

Five men ran out, splashing wildly, urged on by cheers from their female partners waiting in the boats, hopped in their boats and began rowing hurriedly.

Rhetta tried to hold the boat steady as Bates hopped in. And it suddenly occurred to her that she was facing him, and would probably have to remain in that position the entire trip unless she wanted to risk toppling the small boat over by turning around.

"I hope your guess is right about this boat," Bates said as they took an early lead.

Rhetta turned her head to the side and looked out at the other boats. Most of them were already falling off as the men were unused to the exercise and were rowing sporadically. Joey Heckenkemper had already pooped out and had turned the rowing over to Kathleen Smith.

Rhetta glanced at Bates's brown chest and watched the way his arm muscles strained with each stroke he took. His chest looked massive and hard. A rivulet of sweat rolled from his neck and down between his pectoral muscles. Rhetta looked away again and pushed her hair off her neck. It was still hot out on the water, with the last light of the sun reflecting off the surface of the lake.

They were about halfway across the lake when Rhetta noticed Bates was turning and heading for the shore to their left. This was not the turn-around point.

"Bates, where are you going?" she asked quietly, her fears and dreams coming true. Bates grinned, as if he divined the conflicting emotions in her.

"Well, Rhetta, the boat is leaking, and unless you want to swim back, we need to get to the nearest shore and bail this boat out before heading back. We're out of the race."

"Oh!" Rhetta looked down at the puddle of water completely covering the bottom of the boat and inching higher. "Oh, dear!" she exclaimed as she looked at the distance to shore.

"We're not going to make it by dark at this rate," he said, noting the sun had disappeared behind the horizon, leaving only dark purple and a faint pink streaked across the sky.

Rhetta looked at Bates, and he grinned, as if he were glad that they had gotten into this predicament. He deftly lifted himself out of the boat and lowered himself into the water.

"Where are you going?" Rhetta called out after him, fearing he would leave her to drift along until she floated to shore.

"I'm going to push us to shore." Bates began kicking with his feet, pushing the boat ahead of him, and Rhetta decided that he was right; they were making much faster progress than they had when he was paddling, with the boat so full of water and his added weight.

Rhetta reached out and cupped some water in her hand to splash on her neck and shoulders. The air was still warm, and the water looked so cool and inviting.

"When we get to shore, we can take a swim," Bates offered.

"I'm about ready for one," Rhetta agreed. Her skin felt sticky, and she noted that they were very close to land.

Bates finally touched bottom, and after the water became fairly shallow Rhetta hopped out of the boat and helped him pull it up onto the beach. They were in a small bay that hooked out a little bit before coming back around, partially secluding them from the rest of the lake.

Bates released the oars, propped them against a rock, and then he tipped the boat over and let the water pour out.

The rowboats had touched the other shore and several teams had started back across the lake. She could hear faint shouts, and she waved to the other boaters as they went past and then sat down on the beach to wiggle her toes in the sand.

"It's nice here," she said, noticing that neither one of them had suggested getting right back in the boat and heading safely back to the picnic.

"Yes, it is," he agreed as he settled down on the sand beside her. Bates rested his hands on his knees and looked out over the water, which was growing darker as the twilight faded into night.

"Sometimes when I was a little girl, I used to think that I wanted to sail around the world. Go clean away from Tuckerville," Rhetta mused.

"Really?" Bates looked at her with raised brows, thinking she appeared beautiful in any kind of light. "That strikes me as a little too adventurous for Rhetta Tucker."

"Well, I guess actions speak louder than words. I'm still here and I've never sailed around the world. But a part of me still wants to do that. Someday." Rhetta sighed and stared out at the stillness of the lake.

"When?"

"When I've finished my work here in Tuckerville," she answered promptly, and turned to face him.

"When will that be? You can't finish something like a town, can you?"

"Sure you can." Rhetta leaned back on her hands. "Not in the sense that you finish a project or a building or something like that, but you can get a town to where it doesn't need you anymore—to a point where there are two or three others that can step in and take your place."

"I guess you're right. After all, America has survived pretty well with a new President every four years. I would imagine Tuckerville could too."

"Are you thinking of applying for my job next election?" she asked, teasingly.

"No way." Bates shook his head emphatically.

"Why not? I thought you said I was doing a terrible job." Rhetta cupped her hand and let the sand trickle through her fingers.

"Rhetta, you should know me well enough now to realize that I think many of the improvements you've made in Tuckerville have been vital to bringing my company here in the first place. We just disagree on how to proceed from here." Bates grinned.

"True." Rhetta smiled back at him, and for the first time, felt really good with Bates. Relaxed and comfortable. They were actually having a conversation instead of an argument.

"This is where Justus used to take me fishing when I was a boy," Bates said.

"Really? I've never been to this bay before. 'Course it's not often that old Jonas allows a church picnic— or any other picnickers—on his private shoreline. So," she finished, "we never did come to the lake too often."

"What? None of your dates in high school ever took you on moonlight boat rides?"

"No," Rhetta said softly, "they never did."

"Well, we need to make up for lost time. Come on, let's go for a swim." Bates took her hand, pulling her to her feet, and led her out to the edge of the water.

"Wait a minute," Rhetta said suddenly. "I need to take off my sundress."

"That would be nice," Bates said, grinning.

Rhetta felt a churning heat in her stomach as she removed her cotton shift and tossed it onto a nearby rock. She walked quickly into the water, not meeting Bates's eyes.

"Oh," she said breathlessly when the cool water slid up her skin. "Oh, this feels good." Rhetta swam out a few strokes to where she couldn't touch bottom anymore and then dove under to wet her hair. When she came back up, she couldn't see Bates anywhere.

The moon reflecting off the surface of the water made the lake look black and bottomless. Rhetta looked up at the full August moon. It was fat and golden and sensual, and as she looked at it, Rhetta felt something tugging her heartstrings—and her foot.

She managed to take a short breath before Bates pulled her under. His hands slid up her legs, over her hips and settled on her waist as they emerged together. They both let out soft bursts of air, and Rhetta could see his white teeth gleaming in the moonlight as he smiled. He pulled her closer against his body, and Rhetta became aware of her legs rubbing fleetingly against his muscular thigh. The water lapped about his shoulders, and Rhetta realized he could touch bottom.

"Hey, that's not fair," she said, her voice suddenly low and husky. "You can touch."

Bates squeezed her closer. "Mmmm, I sure can," he said, and slid his hands down her back so that Rhetta was forced to hang on to his shoulders.

A silken awareness filled Rhetta, and she felt heat creeping slowly through her body, like a warm tide coming in. Her eyes sought his in the glow of the moonlight, sensual tension tightening her stomach. His eyes a smoldering blue, he watched her lips part, and slowly, he lifted his eyes to look into hers. The consuming heat of desire was in his eyes and in his kiss when his lips took hers.

With a mindlessness that seemed to drag her into the depths of desire, Rhetta allowed him to take her sweet, wet lips. Slowly nibbling with a maddening sensuality, he caught her lower lip between his teeth and sucked gently, then let it slide out slowly only to take it back again, with the same languorous ease.

Rhetta drove her fingernails through his thick curls, and the wet texture of his hair and skin caused the tide of heat to rise still higher. He pulled his head away and Rhetta looked up at him, dazed, as if she hadn't quite awakened from a dream. Tiny droplets of water clung to his face, and Rhetta wanted to press her lips against each one of them.

"Hang on," he said, and pushed off to reach water that was about waist-high for Rhetta. His leg parted her legs sinuously, and he lowered her to sit with parted legs on his thighs as he crouched down so that the water supported him, as if he were sitting on a chair. A tremor of intense longing quaked through Rhetta.

"I want to feel you against me, Rhetta," he murmured huskily. Bates put his arms around her and pulled her against his hard torso. The contact was nearly her undoing; a fire so hot and demanding shot through Rhetta that it made her ache to press herself closer to him.

His breathing was heavy and short, and his hands ran slowly along her spine, pressing small places on her back firmly, pressing her breasts against his hard-muscled body.

The springy hairs on his chest rubbed against the thin material of her swimsuit, and Rhetta was aroused to the point of mindless abandon by the difference in textures. She dropped her head back in ecstasy, moaned and closed her eyes as he continued his tantalizing movements.

Bates looked at her face. Her neck was arched back like a swan's. The planes of her face were highlighted and shadowed by the blue light of the moon. Her lips were murmuring indistinguishable sounds as Bates watched the pulse at the base of her neck throb rhythmically. At that very moment Bates thought he had never seen her more beautiful, had never seen any woman so beautiful as Rhetta.

When she brought her head forward to look at him, her eyes were hidden by the shadows, but he could see their pale glimmer half-lidded with desire. The air was punctuated with soft, breathy panting as he reached up and ran his hands over her full, heavy breasts, still holding her gaze. This time it was Bates who closed his eyes and dropped his head back as he continued his exploration of her body. His fingers danced over her breasts, creating a whirlwind of sensation in Rhetta. She ran her hands along his chest, her fingernails tracing his muscles down to the waist of his swimming trunks. She hugged him to her, fiercely. Wanting him. All of him.

"Oh, God, Rhetta," he breathed, and then took her lips. A fierce, swift heat wrapped itself around Rhetta and sucked her into an abyss of sensations. Only sensations.

His lips were demanding, coaxing, maddening, until Rhetta could only feel. She could think of nothing but the hard muscles beneath her fingers, his warm mouth closing over hers and his tongue entering and retreating in entreaty. Rhetta needed no invitation; she could feel his desire in every pore of her skin, with every breath she took.

"Oh, God!" he said roughly, lifting her up out of the water as he stood, hugging her body close to his. The night air cooled the water on her skin, making her more sensitive to his warm touch. He carried her up to the shore, then lowered her onto the soft sand.

He covered her body with his, and a swift tremor passed through Rhetta as she felt all of him over her. Heavy and masculine, he was made for her; everything fit as a man and woman were intended to fit together. He covered every inch.

His lips rolled onto hers again and then moved away to explore the curve of her neck, sending ripples of desire dancing along her skin.

The moon glowed softly over them, making his skin darker and richer than Rhetta had ever imagined in her fantasies. She ran her hand over his shoulders, and her hand looked like white porcelain against the bronze of his skin.

Pine trees were rustling slightly in the distance, and Rhetta could smell their faint scent as Bates moved lower and placed his mouth over her breast through the swimsuit material. Rhetta shuddered. She was quickly losing her bearings, losing her mind to this man whose skill as a lover left the Tuckerville boys far behind.

"Bates. Wait. Stop. I need to—stop." Rhetta sat up and tried to catch her breath and gain control of her senses.

"I don't want to stop. I want to—"

"Shhh. Listen." Far on the opposite shore, they heard a hymn being sung. A sweet, melancholy hymn that floated over the quiet water to their ears. Rhetta caught her breath.

What was the matter with her? Was she insane? Everyone would be waiting for them when they returned. It didn't take that long to bail the water out of a boat. They'd all know. How could she? Especially at a *church* function. She had lost her mind.

"We've got to go," she said briskly, standing up and trying to brush the sand off her damp skin.

"Just wait a min—"

"No. I want to go now. Either you take me or I'll leave you here and row myself back," she said shakily.

Bates watched her for a moment silently. Rhetta continued trying to brush the sand off her back and legs, but it clung, sticking to her wet skin like adhesive.

Rhetta marched over and picked up her shift, already regretting her impetuous actions. How could she have forgotten what a Romeo he was? This was incredible. *She* was incredible. Incredibly stupid.

Bates got to his feet slowly, as if in pain. He turned the boat back over and refastened the oars, his face set and grim. Wordlessly he pushed the boat to the edge of the shore, floating it out a ways, and then held it steady for Rhetta.

Rhetta marched out to the boat and shoved her cotton shift onto the seat.

"Get in," he ordered grimly.

Rhetta stole a quick glance at him and then wished she hadn't. He was disgusted with her. And, if the truth were known, she was pretty disgusted with herself. She stepped gingerly into the boat, this time facing the front.

Bates pushed off and then hopped in. The boat rocked beneath his weight. He picked up the oars and began rowing with powerful strokes.

The wind picked up outside the cove and Rhetta felt chilled. Sand dug into her bottom as she sat on the seat shivering, with the wind blowing her hair back from her face and the moon lighting a silvery path through the water. She brushed some of the sand off, and then, mentally shrugging her shoulders, she slipped her shift on over her still-wet swimsuit.

Up ahead she could see the awning lighted by lanterns and could hear them begin the slow version of "Amazing Grace." By the time she and Bates had reached the shore, the picnickers had started singing a spirited rendition of "I've Been Redeemed."

Rhetta knew she must look like she'd been doing exactly what she *had* been doing, so she attempted to brush the sand out of her hair. Why hadn't she rinsed off in the water?

She was too distracted to notice that Bates's good humor had returned. Bates grinned and folded his arms across his chest as he watched her frantic ministrations.

He couldn't wait until everyone noticed their reappearance. He knew that she'd wilt under all the teasing they were sure to receive. And she'd kill him if she ever discovered that he'd known before they'd started out that the shiny red boat had a terrible leak in it. Justus had told him.

When they arrived at the awning, where everyone had gathered, as Bates had expected, there was a lot of teasing.

"Well, Rhetta, where did you two run off to?" Arched eyebrows.

"Did you go digging for buried treasure?" A firm nudge in the ribs.

"Hey, Bates? Did you tell Rhetta you didn't know how to steer the boat?" Raucous laughter.

Rhetta tried to smile and joke back, but it was hard when Bates just stood there with his arms crossed insolently across his chest, his blue eyes dancing in lively amusement, grinning at her distress. He actually seemed to be enjoying himself.

Rhetta felt as if she were back in high school and everyone knew they had been doing something but just "how far" they'd gone was being saved for the men's locker room.

And he probably would brag about it, she thought angrily. But surely a man of thirty-four was more mature than that. Yes, Rhetta conceded, even Bates was more mature than that.

On her drive home from the church picnic, Rhetta tried to steer her mind to other things besides Bates. She noticed that one of the new families that had moved into town in the past month was putting up a brand new chain link fence. And they were keeping the yard much neater than it had been, too.

Rhetta stopped at the corner of Anderson Street and Fifth. A new convenience store was being built there come the first of September—the first one Tuckerville had ever had. Everyone was excited about it. They'd been saying for years that this side of town needed a store. Well, now they'd have one, Rhetta thought as she drove through the intersection. Changes were coming to Tuckerville. Several families had moved to the town over the summer, and children who had grown up and moved away were coming back now that there was steady employment here.

The oak tree on the courthouse lawn would be turning red before long, and the pace would accelerate a little bit as the weather got cooler. Rhetta draped her arm out her car window and opened her hand, as if to catch a little bit of the wind.

This fall she would go camping all by herself and sit quietly in the woods and just listen. Maybe she'd see an owl. She had once, when her family had gone camping when she was very young.

She turned the car into the driveway, hearing the springs creak as the old car dipped when it hit the pothole. Rhetta knew she was home.

Chapter Six

Rhetta pulled her pale blue robe tighter around her waist and yawned sleepily. Plugging in the electric coffee maker, she leaned her elbows on the countertop, sleep still fogging her brain, preventing her from doing anything too mentally strenuous. She yawned again, ran her fingers straight back through her silky hair and then sat down in a chair to wait for the coffee to finish brewing.

Her thoughts rolled over the events of last night at the church picnic. There was something so stimulating about Bates that Rhetta could no more resist his kisses than the moon could resist shining.

Bates's sweet, seductive kisses had the power to make her forget her reservations about him. Rhetta tilted her head to one side and rubbed her arms as she thought of his kisses, his caresses.

Soft lips bent down to nibble on her earlobe, and muscular brown arms encircled her, squeezing her tightly. Rhetta's dreamlike state sharpened into reality as Bates pulled her up into his arms and began a sensual exploration of her lips.

He was dressed in snug-fitting blue jeans and was barefoot and bare chested. His skin was still warm from sleep. Rhetta ran her hands up his muscular arms and tasted the early morning sweetness of his lips.

Bates slid his hand inside her robe and cupped her warm breast. Rubbing in circular motions, his fingers moved closer and closer to the rosy center, and then suddenly he bent over and placed his mouth right over her breast and pulled gently.

Rhetta gasped with pleasure. Slowly, Bates trailed kisses from her breast to her throat, until Rhetta could stand it no longer. She wanted to kiss his lips again. She brought his face up to hers and kissed him as if she couldn't get enough of him, ever.

Rhetta felt as if she were adrift on a sea of sensation that whirled about her like a gentle mist slowly creeping up on her . . . just . . . like . . . last . . . night.

Rhetta pushed out of his arms and, drawing her robe more tightly about her, turned around. Rhetta sensed his anger before she heard it in his voice.

"Damn it, Rhetta," he boomed, whirling her to face him. "You can't keep doing that. What's the matter? Are you afraid Joey Heckenkemper might see you and tell all your busybody friends? What is it?"

"I don't want to do that with you anymore because I don't know you." Her brow knitted in little furrows, and her lips puckered in a frown.

"You what?"

"I don't know you." Rhetta didn't meet his probing gaze.

"I'd say you knew me pretty well last night," Bates said derisively. He folded his arms across the broad expanse of his chest and looked at her.

"That's exactly what I'm talking about," Rhetta said in a huff, pacing in front of him. "I know how you kiss better than I know your personality. And that's not typical of me at all." Rhetta grabbed a cup and poured steaming black coffee into it.

"So what do you want to do about it?" Bates leaned complacently against the counter and faced her.

"I don't know," she said angrily. She blew on her coffee to cool it and took a sip, grimacing when the coffee scalded her.

Walking over to the coffeepot, Bates poured a cup for himself and then shot a glance at her. "Rhetta." He made a fist and then flexed his fingers, as if he were searching for the right words. "I love sex."

Rhetta's clear eyes opened wider, but she said nothing. The man certainly wasn't bashful.

"I consider sex a very healthy, very natural, very vital part of any relationship I have with a woman."

"Bates, we don't even *have* a relationship."

"I thought we did." He seemed momentarily dumbfounded at her dismissal of their time spent together. "The beginnings of one, anyway." He sipped his coffee and his eyes narrowed in contemplation.

"Well, that's it in a nutshell." Rhetta set her coffee cup down abruptly in exasperation. "You think that arguing and kissing is a relationship. For heaven's sake, Bates, we've never even had a date! And you call that a relationship? Ha," she scoffed.

"We've had a date, haven't we?" His black eyebrows pulled together as he searched his memory.

"No. We haven't," Rhetta answered more calmly. She smoothed her hands over her thighs and tied the knot of her robe tighter at her waist in agitation.

"Oh." His gaze darted around the neat, pale yellow kitchen.

"Oh?"

"Well, my God, Rhetta, I haven't asked a girl out on a date in God knows how many years," Bates defended himself. He turned his head away from her and smiled a little to himself.

"No, I don't suppose you have. The kind of woman you're used to usually solicits your company."

Bates grinned at Rhetta's insinuation. "I haven't ever been that desperate. But, no, I usually just meet these women, and then we just kind of see each other until the thrill is gone." He shrugged.

"In bars?"

"What?"

"Do you meet these choice, grade A women in bars?"

"Some of them."

"Mmm." Rhetta nodded her head. A heavy silence followed, and Rhetta watched Bates shifting from one foot to the other.

"All right." He cleared his throat. "Rhetta, will you go out on a date with me?" He looked at her expectantly.

"When?"

"What do you mean, 'when'? You aren't supposed to say that! You're supposed to say, 'Yes, I'd love to, Bates.'"

Rhetta grinned. "Where did you learn that bit of etiquette, from Emily Post?"

"Never mind. Just answer me. Can you go out with me this Saturday night? Yes or no," he said brusquely.

Rhetta eyed him and quickly ran through all the reasons why she shouldn't. Her defenses against the attraction she felt for Bates weren't strong enough to endure four hours alone with him. He was a wanderer. His business would fail and he'd be gone in a year. She didn't like him. "Yes," she answered succinctly.

"I'll pick you up at eight o'clock." Bates turned, took his coffee cup from the counter and walked through the swinging white door, whistling "Some Enchanted Evening."

Rhetta turned and smothered a grin, even though there was no one there to see it.

Bates straightened his tie and looked in the mirror. He ran his fingers along his chin. Smooth as a baby's—well, not quite, he admitted. But it was pretty darned smooth. Running his fingers through his hair, he tried to smooth down some of the unruly black curls, but they kept springing back up. Finally, he gave up. At thirty-four, he might as well accept the fact that he had curly hair.

Bates looked around the room, then slipped his billfold and some spare change into his pocket. Then he took the spare change out again. He didn't want to jingle when he walked. He picked up the bouquet of daisies he'd left on his dressing table and checked his watch. One more minute.

He ran his finger around the inside of his collar and swallowed. Switching off the air conditioner, Bates grabbed his keys and walked out of his room. He walked down the hall, stopped at the second door and knocked brusquely. He heard the door behind him creak open. He turned to see who was so nosy.

"Hello, Miss Lee," he said, greeting the buck-toothed spinster with a stiff smile as she peeked out into the hall.

"Oh! Hello, Bates, darlin'. Why, don't you look sweet." Her milky blue eyes twinkled warmly. "Do you and Rhetta have a date for this evening?" she asked excitedly, clasping her hands together in hope.

"Yes, ma'am. I think so." He rapped again at Rhetta's door, a little harder this time, wondering where in the hell Rhetta was.

"Well, have fun." Miss Lee wiggled her fingers and wrinkled her nose at him before slipping back inside her room.

Bates grinned at her and turned back to Rhetta's door just as she opened it.

"I'm ready," she said, her smile a little tight.

His gaze ran over her quickly. She was wearing a pale peach silk dress. The bodice draped gently over her breasts and was cinched at the waist. The soft peach made her auburn hair look rich and lustrous as it fell in soft curls around her face.

The paleness of her blue eyes was highlighted by a light stroke of glittering, silvery-blue eye shadow that added a sparkle to her eyes.

Bates had always thought that the rest of her face was at odds with those calm blue eyes. Her nose was slender and straight, sensually flaring at the nostrils, set over full and rounded lips that were parted now, waiting.

"These are for you." Bates thrust the somewhat wilted daisies at her.

"Oh. Oh, thank you," she stammered. "Let me put them in some water." She backed into her room, turned around and then turned back suddenly. "I don't have any water up here."

Bates grinned at her as he stood lounging in the doorway, hands stuffed deeply in his pockets. This is going to be wonderful, he thought. *She's* nervous.

Rhetta cleared her throat and walked forward, waiting for Bates to remove himself from the doorway. He backed away, allowing her to precede him down the hallway and the stairs to the kitchen, where she placed the flowers in some water.

Bates glanced at his watch. "I have dinner reservations for eight-thirty. Perhaps we'd better leave now."

"Fine." Rhetta walked down the steps as Bates pulled the back door open for her and held it. "Is your car parked out front?"

"Yes. These modern boarding houses don't have garages for their boarders," he teased. She managed another tight smile.

Rhetta walked a half-step ahead of him to the car. His leisurely gait was making her nervous. What was the matter with her? She was usually so calm and self-possessed.

The car door was locked, so Rhetta had to stand and wait, enduring his amused scrutiny while he unlocked the door and finally opened it for her.

"Thank you." Rhetta slid into the car. This was going to be a very difficult evening. This date was a big mistake.

Bates got in beside her. "I hope you like the restaurant I selected. Of course, it's nothing like the restaurants they have in Dallas or Houston, but it's got a solid reputation locally."

"I'm sure it will be fine," Rhetta said primly as he started the car and shifted into gear. There were only a couple of restaurants near Tuckerville that even required a coat and tie. That narrowed the possibilities substantially. She assumed they were going to Crane's, an exclusive restaurant in Jasper.

The traffic along the gray highway lined with tall pine trees was practically nonexistent. Rhetta could see that the moon was beginning to show, but it was just a sliver in the darkening Texas sky.

Neither of them said much during the drive to the restaurant, but Rhetta was very aware of the number of times his dark gaze strayed to her profile.

They didn't go to Crane's after all. They went to a newer restaurant that Rhetta had never been to before. Had never before even heard of. Clancy's. When she saw the outside of the restaurant, she assumed Bates was playing a dirty trick on her. It looked like a barbecue joint. But when they entered, Rhetta was relieved to see that most of the diners were wearing dresses or suits and that the furnishings were very nice, in a simple way. Nothing flashy or fancy, but elegant in its simplicity.

A man walked forward to greet them. "Batesy, how are ya, boy?" He stuck out his hand and slapped Bates on the back.

"Well, pretty good, Jack." Bates grinned. "Jack, I'd like you to meet my landlady, Rhetta Tucker." Bates winked at her, but Rhetta failed to see anything funny in his remark. Jack laughed heartily, though.

"Rhetta Tucker. Well it's surely nice to meet you, hon'. You aren't Poog Tucker's daughter, are you?"

"Yes, I am. The last of the Tuckers." Rhetta smiled at him, liking his hospitable manner.

"Well, I'll be. Poog was a mighty fine man. Mighty fine," Jack said, shaking his head in admiration. Rhetta's chest swelled. She was pleased that Jack had said in front of Bates what a fine man her father had been. She'd always felt that Bates thought her family were a bunch of no-accounts who'd ruined Tuckerville.

Jack seated them at a window table with fresh carnations and a candle. Very romantic.

"They seem to know you quite well here," she said as a dinner-conversation starter.

"I've brought a few of my potential customers and a couple of my management staff here to get better acquainted."

"Oh, that's very nice." She smoothed her napkin in her lap and picked up the menu. He's certainly throwing around a lot of good money, considering he owes so much to the bank that his business isn't really his at all, she thought to herself. Treating his clients to pork chops at Faye's would have served the same purpose. She grudgingly admitted, though, that the atmosphere at Faye's wasn't very conducive to pushing business deals through.

"Let's see," he mused, recalling his manners as a date. "I can recommend the chicken kiev, the charcoaled lamb chops, ummm, the lobster.... There's really not anything that I wouldn't recommend." Bates looked at her composed face, and suddenly he wanted to end this farce, to just be the old Rhetta and the old Bates. This wasn't going to be any fun.

"Thank you." Rhetta looked down the price list, and she selected the least expensive item on the menu. He might be a spendthrift, but as mayor of Tuckerville, she could certainly show him how to run a business more economically.

The waiter approached their table. "Would you care for a cocktail before dinner?"

"Rhetta?" Bates asked politely.

"No thank you. My water's just fine." She picked up her glass and took a drink, as if to show Bates that she loved water.

"Just bring us a bottle of that Codorniu champagne." He'd never known a woman who'd refuse champagne.

"Very good," the waiter murmured approvingly. "And has the lady decided upon her dinner selection?"

"I'll have the chicken," she said promptly.

"And you, sir?" The waiter stood poised, awaiting Bates's answer.

Bates looked amused by Rhetta's choice, as if he knew why she had ordered the chicken. "I'll have the lobster, thank you." Bates returned their menus to the waiter, dismissing him with a slight nod of his head.

Bates looked over at Rhetta and laughed. And continued laughing. Rhetta looked at him, at first in puzzlement. Then while watching him laugh, her expression changed to amusement, until she was giggling, too. "What? What's so funny?" she asked.

"This." His arm swept through the room. "All of this. This whole date has been a mockery. When I picked you up, I'll admit, I was a little nervous, but when I saw how nervous *you* were, it all became so comical." He laughed again and Rhetta joined in.

"Well, you were pretty stiff yourself," she said, smiling. "Flowers? From Bates McCabe? You must have been holding them in a death grip. They were nearly wilted."

"Well, I can explain that." He held up his hand to stop her words while he caught his breath after laughing so hard. "As you well know, there is no florist in Tuckerville, so I had to drive over to Pineland. At work, my secretary stuck the flowers in water, and when I left, I just brought them home in a paper towel and stuck them on the dressing table until it was time to go. I'm sorry they were wilted," he added sheepishly.

"Well, I suppose I really can't complain. I mean, you've certainly done everything according to the book." She smiled, picked up her water goblet by the stem and ran her thumb down the heavy cuts in the glass.

"Yeah, but it hasn't come naturally."

"So what are we going to do now?" she asked.

"What do you mean?" Bates stretched his long legs out in front of him, and his hands came together to form a steeple.

"Well, if dates don't come naturally to you..."

"I didn't say dates didn't come naturally to me. It's just this kind of date that bothers me. It's all so prescribed." There was a lengthy pause. Bates stole a quick glance at Rhetta. "What do *you* think we should do?"

"Mmm. Well, I know I'm attracted to you." Rhetta kept her eyes downcast and toyed with her birthstone ring.

"And I damned well know I'm attracted to you."
Bates paused as the waiter appeared with their champagne.

The waiter started to go through the motions of
having Bates approve it, but Bates waved him away
after the waiter had uncorked the bottle. "That always makes me feel so damned silly," he said, referring to the wine-approval ceremony. Bates poured the
sparkling wine into the champagne flutes himself and
then recorked the bottle, returning it to the silver ice-bucket by their table. "Well, here's to mutual attraction," he said, his blue eyes dancing gaily at Rhetta's
wary look as he raised his glass in a toast.

She toasted and took a small sip. "Mmm, that's
good." She hiccuped. "Excuse me. Champagne always does that to me."

"Sure." Bates looked at her, waiting for her to
continue their previous conversation. "Well?" he
prompted when she remained silent.

"I guess what bothers me is that I feel like we're
going in two different directions. I mean, now we've
cleared the air and admitted we're both attracted to
each other in the physical sense, right?"

"Right," he admitted, and leaned back in his chair,
waiting for her to continue.

"So, where do *you* want to go from here?"

"Honestly?" He grinned.

Rhetta nodded her head.

"To bed." He sat back and waited for her reaction.

"That's exactly what I'm talking about. Your next
step in building a relationship is into the bedroom,

mine is to spend more time getting to know one another." She looked at him for understanding and
paused as the waiter delivered their meal.

"Rhetta," Bates said as he picked up his fork and
knife, "you'd be very surprised how well you can get
to know someone in bed."

"Shhh." She glanced furtively around the room.
"That short-circuits the relationship, and you know it.
You stop communicating and solve all of your problems with sex. Since we hardly communicate at all except by arguing, going to bed together would be
absolutely disastrous in our case." Rhetta sliced into
her chicken with a decisive motion and took a bite.

"Sex *is* a form of communication, Rhetta. And it
could be very good between us. I can feel it."

Rhetta sighed heavily. "I've no doubt you're right,
Bates, but I am *not* going to base a relationship on sex.
That's a terrible foundation to build on."

"Don't you ever just relax and have a good time
without all this analysis? You sound like a therapist,"
he said derisively.

"No, I don't," she said calmly. "I've worked very
hard at gaining the respect of the community. While
that may not mean much to you, I'm aware that as
mayor, I need to set a good example for the youth of
Tuckerville. I'm not about to ruin all of that. And
don't tell me that no one would find out, because you
know what a small town Tuckerville is and how
everyone gossips."

"So you're refusing to sleep with me, even though
you want to, on the grounds that somebody might find

out. In other words, you would sleep with me if you knew no one would ever find out, is that right?'' he asked softly.

"No. No, that's not right. You're just twisting my words," she said angrily. "I won't go to bed with you because I don't think our relationship as friends has advanced far enough." Rhetta's silverware clattered in the steady din of conversation in the crowded restaurant.

"So if I see you more and we become friends, then will you sleep with me?" he asked silkily.

"I think this conversation has gone far enough." She picked up her champagne and drank more than she had intended, then set the glass down abruptly as the sparkling wine coursed through her body.

"On the contrary, Rhetta, it hasn't gone far enough. I need to know that you aren't just stringing me along. You've led me to the brink quite a number of times now, Rhetta." Bates finished off his champagne, poured some more into her glass and then refilled his own.

"I'm not a tease. I know that's probably what it's seemed like to you, but it's just not true. I got carried away, that's all. Just like you." Rhetta folded and refolded her napkin in her lap and reached up to touch the carnations.

"So, will you continue to see me?" Bates shoved his hands in his pockets and watched her.

"I'd—I'd like to, but…" Rhetta took a deep breath and met his gaze squarely. "But I want to slow down the physical side of our relationship."

Bates sat forward and took another sip of his champagne. "I had a feeling those would be the terms," he muttered. "So you're saying that you want to get to know me better and, after you do, then..."

Rhetta looked warningly at him.

Bates laughed at her expression and picked up her hand and kissed it. "All right. I think we understand one another now."

"Yes," she said, coolly, "I believe we do."

Chapter Seven

Fall had come to the piney woods, and hence Senator Hawkins was on the campaign trail again. Senator Hawkins was a big man with thick white hair and a seemingly perpetual tan. The one time Rhetta had met him, she'd felt that his assessing glance from behind his gold wire-rimmed glasses had taken her measure in a matter of moments. He had a bulbous nose, a lumbering gait, and when he stood, his knees dipped in toward each other, which called to Rhetta's mind an image of him as a chubby boy of twelve with pudgy knock-knees and a wide smile that he still wore when politicking.

He was making a thirty-minute stop in Tuckerville just to see how their town was progressing. Rhetta was to guide him through the town and show him the improvements they were making.

"It's probably the most exciting thing that has ever happened in Tuckerville," Nanny was saying to her, making Rhetta feel even more nervous.

"I'm excited about it," Rhetta agreed, stamping the due date in the last book in Nanny's pile, then checking the clock once again. She was closing the library early today so she could make it over to the courthouse on time to meet the senator.

"Well, are you going to take your car, Rhetta?" Nanny leaned across the desk and peered at the statistics Rhetta was going over.

"Hmmm? No, he has a car." She stopped studying the statistics and looked up at Nanny. "Could you honestly imagine a big man like Senator Hawkins even sitting in my little car, let alone riding around town in it for thirty minutes? It would be disgraceful."

"Well, I guess that's right." Nanny chuckled. "You planning on recitin' all those statistics to him? I wouldn't." She shook her head emphatically.

Rhetta remained silent and tried to ignore her.

"No, ma'am, I sure wouldn't. Not after what I learned about the psychology of politicians." Nanny perched herself on the edge of Rhetta's desk, her black shoes dangling off the floor.

Rhetta sighed. It couldn't be helped. "What did you learn about the psychology of politics?" she asked mechanically.

"Not *politics*, child, *politicians*. There's a whale of a difference, too." Nanny fixed her with one of her listen-to-me-'cause-I-know-what-I'm-talking-about looks. "According to an article I read in the *Weekly Express*, politicians have the worst memories, and that's why they have to have all those aides running around tellin' them what to say."

"Did Eustus T. Boner write that article, Nanny?"

"Well, yes, I believe he did."

Rhetta stopped listening to what Nanny was saying. Eustus T. Boner was a kook as far as Rhetta and half the town were concerned and shouldn't be on a newspaper, where people could read his crazy ideas.

"Well, Nanny, I've got to go now. I'll see you in a couple of hours." Rhetta shut her notebook in a dismissive manner and picked up her purse and keys.

"All right." Nanny followed her to the door, tapping her blue flowered umbrella on the floor as she walked. "Now don't forget. If you want someone to remember something, tell it to his aide."

Rhetta didn't bother to explain that Senator Hawkins was only a state politician and probably wouldn't be traveling with his aides. "Thanks, Nanny." Rhetta waved and hurried down the street, the wind whipping her hair up and propelling her forward. Turning the corner to enter the courthouse on the south side, she noticed the newly refurbished fountain had been drained because of the cooler weather. The Development Committee wasn't going to take any chances on a freeze cracking the fountain this winter.

Pulling open the tall white door to the courthouse, she walked inside, her footsteps making a scratchy, hollow sound as she crushed tiny granules of sandy dirt on the marbled floor. She walked swiftly down the hall, turned left and stopped at the door with Mayor printed on it in large, black letters. She noted that the door was unlocked. Justus had probably come to find something.

"Oh, hello." Rhetta paused, once inside her office, attempting to smooth down her wind-blown hair. "I didn't think you'd be here this soon," Rhetta stammered.

Senator Hawkins was seated in a low, forest-green chair. Its fake leather covering was cracked in places, but the chair was still functional. He stood when Rhetta entered the room, as did Justus, who had been seated beside him.

"No problem. Justus has been entertaining me with some pretty good stories." Senator Hawkins slapped Justus on the back jovially.

"Oh, well, I'm glad he's kept you entertained," Rhetta said, hoping Justus hadn't spread a bunch of idle gossip. Especially about her.

"Oh, believe me, he has." The senator's eyes twinkled at her, and Rhetta's hopes were dashed. Justus Burns must have told him how she and Bates had come to a deadlock over Bates's computer-manufacturing plant. The old coot, she thought.

"Well," she said, taking a deep breath. "Are you ready to leave now? I know you must be in a hurry, so we'll wrap this up quickly." Rhetta gripped her notebook and clenched her purse strap tightly in her hand. She was going to kill Justus. Later.

"Sounds good, Rhetta." He turned to the older man. "Justus, look me up when you're down at the capital and you can let me know how my mayor's doing." He winked at Rhetta as he said this.

Justus had the grace to look sheepish. His watery brown eyes looked anywhere but at Rhetta. "You two go on, now. I'll lock up," he said gruffly. Justus shoved the senator out the door with Rhetta. Rhetta shot Justus a parting look that said she'd deal with him later.

"I thought that first we'd go on a walking tour of the downtown area." Rhetta skirted an old piece of pink bubble gum on the sidewalk and headed south along Brick Street. "I'm glad you brought your jacket. The wind's a little brisk today."

"Wooo! That breeze is pretty stiff." Senator Hawkins buttoned his suit coat and kept up with the quick pace Rhetta was setting, pulling his light gray stetson down lower.

"You'll probably be very interested in the building next to Faye's. Sarah Long has set up a baby-clothes manufacturing plant in there and business has been so good that she's moving out next month to a larger building north of town." Rhetta looked with pride at the newly painted building with the shiny glass windows. This was the new Tuckerville. "Her business has doubled every two months since she's been open. Her biggest problem is keeping up with her orders." Rhetta waved to a harried Sarah, who was looking out of a window, and Senator Hawkins saluted Sarah in military fashion.

"Right next to her is a shoe store that just opened up. People used to drive to Pineland or Jasper for shoes, but now they're able to shop here at home. The most significant aspect of all of this is that for the previous ten years, these buildings have been vacant because Tuckerville simply didn't have an economy healthy enough to support them." Rhetta kept walking, but Senator Hawkins stopped abruptly in the middle of the sidewalk.

"Well, Rhetta, it sounds like y'all are going great guns down here. What I mean to say is—" he took a politician's stance, and gestured extravagantly "—a mayor that cares about his town—pardon me, her town—can do a great deal of good for her people. A mayor who cares, I mean really cares, can make her town profitable no matter what the odds. There's a lot of people who'd like to be mayor, but they'd just use Tuckerville and not give anything back. That's not what Tuckerville needs." His gray eyes looked piercingly at Rhetta. "I believe you've got it, Rhetta. Tuckerville needs you." He pointed his finger at her. "Tuckerville needs your guidance and drive. And I need you down here doing a good job for our district." He relaxed his stance and smiled at her.

"Thank you." Rhetta smiled, but inwardly she was worried. She'd been hearing things through the grapevine—things that worried her in a way she had not anticipated. She pushed her anxieties to the back of her mind and continued with the tour. "Two new dress shops will be opening up downtown in time for Christmas. For the first time since I can remember,

Tuckerville is *looking* prosperous," Rhetta said with more enthusiasm than she was feeling.

They finished the tour of downtown, got into the senator's car and drove out to Steven's tool-manufacturing plant, which from all reports, was stable and steady.

When they arrived, Rhetta said, "This is Steven Sutphen's tool-manufacturing plant." As they drove slowly by, she added, "You know his father, don't you, Senator?"

"Sure do. He's a fine man. Fine man." He shook his head for emphasis. "What's this building here?" He stopped the car and pointed to an aluminum-sided oblong building directly across from Sutphen's tool-manufacturing plant.

"Oh, that's where Sarah's new baby-clothes factory will go. It's real nice on the inside." Rhetta followed his gaze to the pale yellow building set in among towering pine trees and decided it didn't look at all like a typical manufacturing plant. It was friendly and pure Sarah.

"Now let's drive out to see Bates McCabe's place. Justus says it's really something." He turned the car around and headed down the highway toward Bates's plant.

I'll just bet he did, she thought, feeling once again that Justus had railroaded her into seeing Bates. Rhetta got a sinking feeling in the pit of her stomach. She didn't want to see him. They drove the short distance in silence.

"This is it, Senator. You have to turn in or you can't see it very well." Perhaps they wouldn't go in, she thought hopefully.

"Sure are a lot of cars here," he observed as they bounced along the graveled drive.

"He has a lot of employees," Rhetta commented noncommittally.

"Let's take a peek inside. I'm sure Mr. McCabe won't mind." Senator Hawkins parked his flashy silver Cadillac and got out. "Ah, that feels good," he said, stretching his legs. "Sure is pretty out here." The wind whipped the tails of his suit coat back behind him, and he held on to his hat with one hand as he surveyed the land surrounding Bates's plant.

"Yes," Rhetta said as she joined him, "it is." For some reason a lump came into her throat when she looked over at Kern's Hill, which had been named after one of Faye's ancestors. The smell of autumn was in the air, and to Rhetta, Tuckerville was never more beautiful than in the fall. She looked back over at Bates's manufacturing plant, and little worry lines etched themselves on her forehead. Without another word, Rhetta led the way into the plant.

It was noisy inside, with the sound of machinery whirring, buzzing and, occasionally, clanging. Men were yelling instructions and walking to and fro. A young woman was hunched over a computer component that looked like the inside of a transistor radio.

Rhetta turned and walked toward Bates's office. There was a big glass window covered by a miniblind that had been hung cockeyed and partially obscured the view so that she could only see Bates from the waist down. His fist was banging on his desk, and Rhetta could see the telephone cord stretching up, then out of view behind the blind. There was a rapid series of expletives and a loud bang when Bates slammed the receiver down.

Rhetta smiled a little as she opened the door to his office without knocking. Something akin to guilt and defensiveness replaced his anger when he saw Rhetta. "What do you want?" he asked bluntly.

Rhetta smiled fondly at his "warm" greeting. Professionalism first, she reminded herself. "Senator Hawkins has heard a lot about your operation from Justus and the others who so frequently sing your praises. He wanted to meet you before he left town." Rhetta stepped forward, allowing Senator Hawkins to enter Bates's office.

"Oh." Bates tried to straighten his tie, then quickly reached to shake Senator Hawkins's outstretched hand.

"I've heard a lot about you, son." He patted Bates on the back warmly. "I hear this plant is only the beginning, that you plan to build others—perhaps also in Texas?" he wheedled.

"I really haven't thought that far into the future, Senator," Bates said noncommittally.

"Well, let me know if I can be of any help," the Senator continued. "Justus thinks you've done wonderful things for Tuckerville, and by the sound of it, you've become a regular town hero."

"Thank you, Senator." Bates sighed tiredly. "I hope I can continue to please the residents of Tuckerville and not disappoint them. Times are tight in the computer industry."

Rhetta's stomach dropped and her eyes sought Bates's, but he wouldn't look at her. The rumors she'd heard weren't just rumors. Bates's business was in trouble.

Bates gave them a brief tour of his operation and they left.

Standing at the window of his office, he watched Rhetta walk away, and for once, Bates really hurt. Rhetta knew. He'd seen it in her eyes—eyes that he had never been able to read before.

She'd probably heard that his sales figures were way down. Rumors were bound to have gotten around. And she'd be the most likely candidate for someone to tell.

Although God knew he'd wanted to, Bates hadn't seen Rhetta much lately. He'd been trying to pull his sales up. But the contracts still weren't coming in. Business was slow, sluggish, and that was bound to be felt by his employees.

Bates turned away from his window and sat down at his desk. Rubbing his eyes, he buzzed his secretary. "I'll be in the design area if you need me."

He'd been working on his new design more and more, hoping that it would be the key to the company's success. It was a big risk for a fledgling company to take, but it was the only way.

If sales didn't pick up, he'd be bankrupt in six months. And Rhetta would have been right about his business, after all. And for some reason, it bothered him more to disappoint her than anyone else in the world.

Bates rubbed the back of his neck and then headed out the door.

Rhetta breathed in the cool fall air and dropped the quilt on the ground. "This is it," she said with finality.

"Are you sure?" Bates asked dryly. "We've been going around in circles for an hour, and we must have been to this spot at least three times."

"We have not. I know these woods like the back of my hand." Rhetta walked over and took the picnic basket from him and placed it on the ground near their feet. "Stop being such a grouch." She touched his nose playfully with the tip of her finger and noticed the heavy lines of exhaustion beneath his eyes and around his mouth. "You need to get away from the office once in a while."

Bates walked around her and picked up the quilt. The office was one subject he couldn't talk about right now.

He kicked several brown spiky pinecones away from their picnic area and flapped the quilt open. The pink-and-white checked cloth sailed up into the air and then settled back down neatly on the forest floor, cushioned by thousands of pine needles.

Rhetta brought the picnic basket over and sat down. She opened her mouth to say something and then shut it again.

Talk about Bates's business had been running rampant through Tuckerville lately, and Rhetta was now seen as a kind of oracle, a Cassandra whose prophecies had not been heeded in time.

And oddly enough, she didn't want to be seen as the one who had forecast the failure of Bates's business. She didn't want the residents to see her that way nor for Bates to see her that way. She wanted to help. She wanted to be his friend.

"Are you ready to eat yet?" Rhetta flipped up the lid of the basket.

"No, I'm not really hungry right now. I ought to be working." Bates sat down heavily, and the smell of the freshly washed quilt took some of his tiredness away.

"No you shouldn't. I told you last summer I'd take you on a picnic in the fall, and it's nearly winter now." Rhetta rubbed her hands against the light jacket she wore over her teal-blue flannel shirt and shivered. "I know what we need," she said with forced cheerfulness. "Hold this." She took two Styrofoam cups and handed them both to Bates. Retrieving a bottle of red wine from the basket, she quickly uncorked the bottle and poured a generous amount into each cup.

A smile touched his lips. He handed Rhetta her cup and then tipped his softly against hers. "Here's to you." He drank, but Rhetta didn't.

She cocked her head to one side. "That's all?"

"What did you want me to say, 'Here's looking at you, kid'?" He drank again and watched her.

Rhetta pressed her lips together. She smiled, feeling the tingly feeling of numbness from the wine. "Oh, I just expected you to say something more derogatory, that's all." Then Bates smiled, too. Now that's a healthy sign, she thought as she watched his smile widen into a grin.

"Have I really been that bad?"

"Well, let's see. Since our first date, we've had about three more." She raised her finger in the air. "That's over a three-month period. Not exactly a boon to a girl's ego. Once you were introducing me and forgot my name—"

"Now wait a minute. I told you what happened there. That was an old girlfriend, and I had no idea she'd show up here. I was a little disconcerted, that's all."

"And then," she continued, swirling the wine in her cup as she spoke, "you forgot we even had a date. I waited for two hours before calling your office, and when I did, a sexy blonde answered."

"Marilyn is not a sexy blonde, and I told you, something very important came up and I couldn't call—"

"Sure, Bates. I realize how important my friendship is to you."

"It *is* important to me, Rhetta," he said quietly as he stared down at his cup.

Rhetta didn't want him to become serious; she wanted him to relax and enjoy himself and not think about the office. "Come on, lazy bones," she chided as she rose to her feet. "You get a fire going, and I'll lay out our lunch."

Bates stood up and looked down at her. "Rhetta?"

Suddenly Rhetta knew what he was going to say, but she didn't want to hear it. She didn't want to hear any confession that his business was about to fail and that he'd be leaving. As long as he didn't say it, then there was still hope. "Oh, all right," he finally said. "I'll help you get the firewood, but then you have to start it."

They both knew that wasn't what she'd been about to say. Bates had sensed her reluctance to discuss his problems. She probably doesn't want to be bothered, he thought.

Bates walked a few yards and began gathering small sticks, twigs and pinecones for the kindling. He then secured a large log. After placing rocks in a circle and brushing away the dead pine needles surrounding the area, he piled the kindling and the log in the center of the makeshift fireplace.

Rhetta dusted her hands off on her jeans and started pulling things out of the hamper. She'd packed enough food for the entire population of Tuckerville.

Rhetta arranged two plates side by side and then took out a thermos of beef stew, a loaf of French bread that she'd made early this morning and butter. For dessert there was sweet-potato pecan pie or marshmallows and chocolate pressed between graham crackers. There was even some hot coffee to wash it down.

Rhetta looked over at Bates. As he slowly fed the flames, the fire began to crackle and pop. His strong, aggressive features had a coppery hue in the faint glow of the firelight.

Rhetta loved the fall. Smells of campfire and pine in the cold air, a gray wintry sky just perfect for snuggling under the canopy of pines, the soft but startling crunch of leaves and dried twigs when she tromped along through the quiet woods, and the occasional rabbit or deer that darted out ahead when she walked toward a stream.

Bates looked over at her. "I hope you brought some wieners to roast."

Rhetta's face fell. "Oh, no. I didn't. But I brought some marshmallows."

"Graham crackers and chocolate bars?"

"Uh-huh."

"Oh, Rhetta, you've found the key to my heart."

She laughed and refilled his wineglass. "I guess Nanny's known that all along."

"Between the two of you, I'll bet I've gained ten pounds since I came to Tuckerville."

Rhetta looked over at his lean well-muscled physique. She wasn't about to touch that one. "Do you think you could scrounge up two sticks that would be good for roasting marshmallows on?"

"Yes, but let's eat first. I'm starved." Bates sat down next to her and suddenly Rhetta became all thumbs. She dropped the bowls and then spilled the stew on Bates's jeans when she was pouring it.

"I'm sorry." Rhetta put the thermos down, screwed the lid on tightly and tried to find something to wipe the liquid off with.

"Do I make you nervous, Rhetta?" he asked silkily.

Rhetta paused. "Sometimes." She looked up into his eyes and found they were twinkling with amusement. She smiled and handed him a spoon. They ate the soup and the bread and butter accompanied only by the sounds of the woods. Sleek black crows issued their screeching caws, a squirrel occasionally chattered, and a colorful cardinal, just passing through on its trip farther south, gave its call as it went by.

Bates took Rhetta's bowl from her and placed it on the picnic hamper. Rhetta licked her lips in anticipation of what she knew was coming. Of what she hoped was coming. Bates lay back, pulling her down on top of him, and Rhetta released a telltale sigh.

"I've missed you, Rhetta." He reached up and curled her hair on one side behind her ear so that the other side draped forward and then let his hand slide to her neck.

She had never expected to hear Bates McCabe make such a vulnerable statement. Rhetta's eyes moved over his features, as though she was memorizing them one by one. His charcoal-blue eyes were half-lidded as he lay back, staring into her eyes. A smile curved her mouth.

With a gentle tug, he pulled her head forward to meet his lips. His mouth closed over hers, and Rhetta felt that familiar bone-melting sensation, which robbed her of any coherent thought. The tightness in her stomach, as though warmed by the seductive heat, loosened and curled outward through her body to fill every cell with a warm weightlessness.

She spread her fingers across his chest, which was covered by the luxurious softness of a lamb-suede shirt. Slowly she released the top two buttons, revealing a chest still bronzed from the warmer days of fall and covered with curling dark hair.

Bates pressed her closer to him, and his hand slid slowly from her back to her waist, where he found the curve of her hip, and down the side of her thigh. Rhetta felt as if she were on fire. She could still taste the wine on his lips, and his alluring male scent filled her head and made her hunger even greater.

She seemed to be swirling in a churning sea of desire and emotional hunger that could only be assuaged by Bates. She wanted to taste him, touch him, comfort him and love him.

Rhetta had never wanted anyone like this. This deep hunger for him grew each time she saw him, each time he touched her.

She pressed herself more fully against him and had the satisfaction of hearing him moan. He nudged aside her shirt to get access to her delectable throat. Tiny shivers of desire raced through her, leaving her with a warm tingly feeling that spread throughout her body and lingered.

His skin was hot to the touch, and Rhetta wanted to touch all of it. She slid her hand inside his shirt to cover his heart. Her long fingernails traced a path of liquid fire across his chest.

Leaning over him, she kissed his eyelids shut and laid her cheek next to his in a loverlike gesture of surrender, then rolled off him, pulling him on top of her.

"Oh, Bates. Please don't ever leave me." Rhetta sought his lips, but Bates pulled back, hesitating, and then rolled away to sit up a few feet to the side of her.

If she hadn't said that, he could have gone through with it. By God, he wanted to go through with it. He wanted her more than any other woman he'd known. And he'd waited longer for her, too.

"Bates?" Rhetta sat up. "What's wrong?"

He looked up at the pine trees and shook his head. *I might not be here tomorrow, Rhetta. I can't promise you tomorrow. And you're the kind of woman who needs to know that I'll be here in the morning . . . the morning after.*

"Is it because we're here? That you're afraid someone might see us?" she asked hesitantly.

Bates looked over at her. If she only knew how much he wanted her. How her auburn hair and her sweet parted lips seemed to fill his dreams like a heady aphrodisiac that made him want to forget his business, Tuckerville, everything. All he could think about was making love to her. A meager smile curved his lips. "No, Rhetta, I'm not afraid someone will see us."

"Then—then don't you want me anymore?" Even as she asked the question, she knew the answer. He still wanted her. But then why was he turning away from her?

"Good God, Rhetta! How much do you think I can take?" he demanded as he rolled to his feet.

"Bates, I—" She put out her hand, reaching for him.

"Rhetta, there are some things I just can't talk about. Okay?" he demanded.

Rhetta nodded her head and sighed heavily.

"I'm going for a walk. I'll be back in a few minutes," he said gruffly.

Bates stuffed his hands deep in the pockets of his jeans and walked through the woods, crushing pinecones and dead twigs without a thought. He'd never done that before, turned down such a blatant opportunity.

But with Rhetta it was different. She wasn't the kind of woman who he could take to bed and then just walk away from. And that's what he'd have to do if business didn't improve soon.

She'd hate him if he made love to her and then his business went belly up and ruined Tuckerville. And not only Tuckerville. Nanny and Justus had invested their money in his company, too. It wouldn't just be a personal failure; it would be a tragedy for the whole town.

Bates paused in the woods, leaning against the trunk of a massive pine, his heart beating strongly in his chest. His lamb-suede shirt was still open from Rhetta's caresses. He clenched his fists into tight balls of frustration and clamped his teeth together like a vice.

He could make it work and he would! Because he wouldn't ever be able to look at himself in the mirror again if he failed them. And especially if he failed Rhetta.

A crafty, foxlike smile curved Bates's lips. He knew that he had one chance left, that there was one way he could pull his company through—he could finish his invention. But it might cost him more than he'd gain by saving his company; it might cost him Rhetta because he wouldn't be able to see her again until the crisis had passed. He hoped she would be his dessert, his prize money, waiting for him at the end of that dark, lonely tunnel.

"Nanny, could you get that chopping board over there for me? I'm likely to lose my place if I don't keep my mind on what I'm doing." Rhetta ran her finger down the recipe book and continued stirring the sauce on the burner as she read.

The house was warm and cozy with the good smell of wintertime foods wafting from the pots on the stove.

Nanny walked over and retrieved the chopping board with a sly smile on her face. "Have you seen Bates lately?"

Rhetta didn't raise her head, but her gaze darted sideways. "No. I mean I've seen him here at the boarding house. Why?"

"He's working a lot of late hours lately. Could be that's why you can't keep your mind on your cookin'."

Watching Rhetta, Nanny crossed her arms over her ample bosom and leaned against the counter.

"I can keep my mind on my cooking just fine, Nanny," Rhetta said evenly.

Rhetta hadn't seen Bates since a week ago, when they'd gone on the picnic together. She had been hurt that Bates hadn't spared five minutes to see her or talk to her. He rarely came home before midnight anymore, and he never called her at the library, either. He was up in the morning by five o'clock and gone before six.

And Rhetta felt such an intense longing for him that she could scarcely restrain herself from climbing into his bed at night when she heard him tiptoe down the hallway in the early hours of the morning. But she didn't. Because if he didn't want to see her, then she didn't want to see him. She had her pride to think of.

"Maybe you should take something for him to eat down to his office, Rhetta. That's what a landlady's for."

The phone rang before Rhetta could issue the sharp retort that was on her lips. "Could you get that please, Nanny?" Rhetta rolled her eyes. It was bad enough having one matchmaker in town without having Nanny start, too.

Nanny walked to the wall phone and lifted the receiver. "Hello? Yes, ma'am, this is she." There was a lengthy pause, and Rhetta glanced over at Nanny and knew immediately that something was terribly wrong.

Nanny's wrinkled face was chalk white and her hand gripped the phone until her knuckles looked as if the bone would break through the skin. Rhetta dropped the spoon in the sauce and rushed over to her. "What is it? Nanny? My Lord, what is it?" Rhetta's mouth went suddenly dry, and her hand went to her throat.

"I'll be there as soon as I can." She turned to face Rhetta, her face as pale as death. "It's Justus. He's had a heart attack."

Rhetta shut her eyes, as if to stop the tears. He couldn't die. Not dear sweet, matchmaking Justus. He'd been here forever. *O dear Lord, please let him live. I'll be so good if you just let him live.* Nanny needed her to be strong. She couldn't cry.

"Rhetta, can you drive me?" Her wrinkled eyelids quivering, Nanny placed a trembling hand on Rhetta's arm.

Rhetta heard her own heart pounding in her ears, as if from a great distance. She gathered Nanny in her arms and squeezed her tightly. "He'll be fine, Nanny. He'll be just fine. I promise." Her mind raced through the things that needed to be attended to. "Get your handbag and a change of clothes—we may have to spend the night. Where did they take him?" There wasn't a hospital in Tuckerville.

"Jasper." Nanny's voice was low and hoarse, as if her throat had closed up tight. Nanny stood there, her eyes wide open like a little girl's, and Rhetta realized that Nanny was in shock.

"Nanny, I want you to sit down right here." Nanny complied woodenly.

Quickly Rhetta ran some hot tap water while she gathered up some instant coffee, sugar and a mug. She dumped in coffee and three teaspoonfuls of sugar, and stirred vigorously. "Drink this. I'll be right back. Don't you dare move until you drink that entire cup."

Nanny nodded mutely and lifted the cup to take a sip.

Rhetta turned and took the sauce off the burner before dashing up the stairs two at a time. She unlocked her room with the keys she kept on a ring around her wrist and grabbed her purse. Then she went into Nanny's room and dumped a few personal belongings into a small suitcase and dashed back down the stairs.

Nanny was looking brighter, with a little more color in her cheeks. She'd put on her hat and coat and was standing silently by the back door, waiting to go. Wordlessly Rhetta led her down the back steps and to the car.

The trip to the hospital in Jasper didn't take long. Soon, Rhetta and Nanny were parking the car and hurrying into the building.

The brisk pace of the hospital momentarily disconcerted both women. The lights seemed harsh and surreal, throwing a sickly pallor on every face they saw. Rhetta approached the information desk to obtain directions to the intensive care unit, then led Nanny to the elevator at the far end of the corridor, their footsteps reverberating in a discordant clack. Lights on a wall panel blinked a series of codes for emergency calls. Nurses and aides swished by in their crisp whites as Rhetta and Nanny stopped in front of the elevators.

Nanny's lips were pursed together in a thin line, and a muscle in her cheek twitched spasmodically during the elevator ride. As they got off, Rhetta squeezed Nanny's arm. Then finally their steps took them to the waiting room.

Nanny walked immediately to the volunteer staffing the desk to obtain information regarding Justus's condition. Rhetta said a silent prayer of thanks when they were informed that his condition was critical but stable. At least stable.

She led Nanny over to some chairs in a secluded corner to wait for the doctor. "Do you want some coffee, Nanny?" Rhetta asked, spying a coffee urn in the corner.

"Yes, I think I need some." Nanny attempted a smile, but her eyes seemed to have lost their sparkle.

Rhetta returned moments later with two cups of coffee and sat down beside Nanny.

"You know, Rhetta, all my life I thought that I tolerated Justus merely because he was just about the only decent man around." She paused, her blue eyes filling with tears, and she bit her top lip to stop its trembling. "But now I know I really do love him." She whispered the last two words. She swallowed painfully, her eyelids squeezing shut as two tears trickled down the dry lines in her cheeks.

Rhetta swallowed hard. She could stand a child's tears much more easily than she could an older person's—it tore her up to see Nanny in so much pain.

She looked so weak and frail, so vulnerable. Rhetta took Nanny's hand, patted it and held it against her soft cheek.

"Oh, Rhetta," Nanny whispered hoarsely, "don't make the same mistake I have. All these years Justus and I could have been so happy together, and I've thrown it all away. I thought I didn't need him. I thought I didn't need anyone, and I let my pride stop me from marrying him. He's asked me a dozen times, and I always turned him down. The Lord's gonna punish me for that, 'cause I hurt Justus."

"Oh, Nanny, Justus knows you love him, even if you've never said it. We all know it." Rhetta was careful to keep her words in the present tense.

"I hope so, Rhetta, I surely hope so." Nanny bowed her head slowly.

Rhetta's eyes had filled with tears—tears that stung and hurt, for they were tears of shame at her own behavior.

How many times had she ridiculed Bates and his business to the townspeople? It was no wonder they thought she was a Cassandra. She had practically engineered his doom. How badly he must have felt, knowing that she was attracted to him physically but that she wanted him to fail.

And now, when his business was in trouble, what had she done to help? Now that people were openly cutting him on the streets of Tuckerville? The idle gossip was becoming an angry buzz against Bates, but Rhetta had kept her mouth shut even though her feelings had changed.

She did want Bates to do well, not just for Tucker-ville, but for himself. Nanny had been right about her; she had wanted to be seen as the savior of Tucker-ville, and Bates had taken that away from her. She had been too proud to back down and say that she was wrong. And she had been very wrong about Bates and about the computer industry. Now more than ever Bates needed her support, and she had been too proud to break down and give it to him. Let him come to me, she had thought. Rhetta shook her head in disgust. Nanny didn't have a corner on the pride market. Rhetta Tucker would change her ways, too.

Rhetta glanced up as Nanny stood.

A physician in a green surgical uniform approached them. "Miss Fields?"

"Yes?" Nanny answered. She waited for the words she wanted to hear.

"He's doing fine. In fact, he's been asking for you." The doctor sat in a chair, pulled Nanny down beside him and spoke in the soothing, hushed tones of a professional. "It was a mild attack. At this point we don't believe there's been any heart damage, but it's honestly too soon to tell."

"Can I see him?" Nanny asked hopefully.

"Well, technically you aren't family—"

"I've been engaged to that man for forty years. I don't see how you can get any more family than that!" she exclaimed hotly.

Rhetta smothered a smile, relieved both at the news and at the return of Nanny's spirit.

"It won't be for another hour or so, but I'm sure we can arrange for you to see him for a few minutes." The doctor smiled at Nanny, and then his gaze became a bit more interested when he looked over at Rhetta. She smiled aloofly back at him. He rose to his feet.

"When you go back in there, you tell him I'm gonna marry him as soon as he gets out, and *I* won't take no for an answer." Nanny nodded her gray head firmly, her hat sliding forward on her head as she did so.

"Thank God," Rhetta prayed out loud.

"That's exactly what I'm going to do," Nanny said firmly, rising to her feet purposefully. "Come on, they're bound to have a chapel somewhere in this hospital," she muttered.

Chapter Eight

"Well, there's only ten days left until Christmas, Rhetta." Swinging her purse by its strap, Nanny walked in the front door with a spring in her step that was more the norm than the exception these days.

Rhetta was in the parlor, tying maroon ribbons and antique lace around the fresh pine and cedar branches she had cut that afternoon from the trees by the lake. The room was filled with the smell of Christmas and with all the joys associated with it.

"Then I know why you're so happy." Rhetta smiled at Nanny's dancing blue gaze. "The doctor said Justus could come home by Christmas, right?" Rhetta guessed.

"That's right!" Nanny sang. She tossed her hat up in the air and flopped down on the slip-covered rose sofa.

Rhetta stood staring at her in amusement. "Well, I'll be," Rhetta said, laughing and placing her hands on her hips. "I ought to have gotten a picture of that! Justus will never believe me." Rhetta shook her head and Nanny laughed sheepishly.

"Don't you dare tell him. He'll never let me live it down."

"Oh, I think he knows you'll be glad to have him home," Rhetta said wryly. "Last time I was over to see Justus, the nurse told me that you two have been cooing like lovebirds every time she's walked in on you," Rhetta teased, placing a few pinecones in among the greenery.

Nanny sat up and rearranged her clothes and smoothed her wavy gray hair back into place. "Well, to tell you the truth, Rhetta, she's right. I made a promise to God when I went into that chapel the day Justus had his heart attack that I wouldn't ever hold back my feelings from Justus anymore. So when I feel like kissin' him, I do, and when I feel like tweekin' his ear, I do, and when I feel like battin' him over the head with a newspaper, I do that, too."

Rhetta laughed with Nanny and thought how good it was to see her feeling so good. She hadn't seen Nanny like this—ever. Nanny Fields had finally admitted she was in love with Justus, and it made all the difference in the world.

"And that's not all, Rhetta." Nanny jumped up from her chair, her purse spilling to the floor.

Rhetta lighted a candle above the fireplace and shook the match out. "Well?" she prompted when Nanny remained silent.

"If the doctor will allow it, we're gettin' married on February fourteenth!"

"Ohhh!" Rhetta squealed, clasping her hands together. "That's so romantic. Does Bates know?"

"Now how in tarnation would he know when he's either been in Houston or down at that plant of his since summer? Sometimes I think you've lost your mind, child."

Rhetta smiled weakly. It was true. She hadn't seen Bates in nearly a month. Not since that day in the woods when she'd practically thrown herself at him and he'd declined her offer.

Rhetta knew now that it wasn't because he didn't want her that he'd refused her. He was in trouble. His business was floundering, and everybody in town was concerned about it. It was no secret now, and Rhetta was worried most of all.

At Nanny's words, Rhetta decided to go see Bates down at the plant. It had taken her weeks to get up her courage. She'd take him something to eat, as Nanny had suggested a couple of weeks ago. Neighborly. She was going to be there to support him and help him if nobody else would. Because she wanted Bates to stay.

Rhetta knocked on Bates's office door timidly and then, when he didn't answer, knocked a little louder.

There was a muffled exclamation. Then the door flew open and Bates stood before her eyes. But it didn't look like the same Bates at all.

His hair was rumpled and too long, and he looked as if he'd lost about twenty pounds. His white shirt was wrinkled, and his pants looked like they'd been slept in, too.

There were coffee cups strewn all over the floor and a half-eaten ham-and-cheese sandwich curled unattractively on his desk. In the corner an overturned alarm clock ticked loudly and what was obviously his suit coat was rolled in a ball for a pillow. Computer printouts were everywhere.

Rhetta's eyes traveled through the jumbled mess and then up to Bates's face. There was a couple of days' growth of black whiskers on the lower half of his face and dark circles beneath his eyes, which were bloodshot and red-rimmed, as if he'd been drinking for weeks.

Rhetta was horrified. "Bates, why didn't you call me?" she asked, pleadingly. Pushing him aside, she began picking up the paper cups and stuffing them in the trash can.

"What are you doing?" he barked, hands on his lean hips.

Rhetta put down the trash can and the large satchel she was carrying. "I want to help you." Rhetta went up and boldly put her arms around him, hugging him tightly to her. He was stiff at first but gradually loosened.

"Ah," he groaned, as if releasing a wave of tension from his body. "By God, Rhetta, I've missed you." He shut his eyes and just held her to him, feeling the reassuring sound of her heartbeat. "I kept thinking that if I could just get through the next day and the next day, then I'd let myself see you. But then I was afraid that if I saw you, I wouldn't ever let you go and my business would fall apart." He buried kisses in her hair.

But Rhetta pulled back from him and searched his face. "How *are* things?"

Bates shrugged and moved away, not meeting her eyes. "Not good." He breathed in sharply, as if just admitting it to himself. "I can't make payroll this month."

Rhetta's eyes widened involuntarily. Heavens! She'd known it was bad, but she hadn't imagined it was down to that already. "What are you going to do?" Rhetta unfastened the top button of her light coat and sat down on a chair piled high with computer trade journals.

"I guess I'll have to borrow more money from the bank." Bates picked up a sterling-silver letter opener and twirled it between two fingers, then tested the point.

"Do you think they'll loan it to you?" Rhetta swallowed. As mayor, she felt she should at least think about the impact on the town. If Bates's plant closed, it would be very bad for Tuckerville.

"I don't know. They've already offered to loan me the money for the other manufacturing operations that I'd planned." Bates grinned, as if he enjoyed his precarious circumstances. "They've got two choices. They can recall the loan and bankrupt me, or they can stick their necks out a little farther and loan me more money." He sat on the edge of his desk and watched conflicting emotions flicker across Rhetta's face like successive shots on a film strip.

"Will it help? I mean, will you be able to make ends meet if you make payroll this month?"

"All I'm doing right now, Rhetta, is buying time. I'm working on an invention that will rip the market wide open if I can make it work and get it marketed on time. But I'm racing against two other guys who are working on similar inventions. I've got to beat them to the punch to be successful."

"Well . . . how long will it take?"

He shrugged and got up from the edge of the desk. "Who knows? It won't matter in the end. It will only matter if I'm first."

There was a crackling sound from somewhere on his desk. "Mr. McCabe?" A disembodied voice filled the room.

Bates shoved some papers aside to uncover an intercom system. He pushed a button. "Yes, Tom?"

"I need you to look over this new relay switch you asked me to design. I've gotta get home early tonight, or the old lady will have my hide."

"I'll be right there," Bates said briskly. He looked up at Rhetta, and she held up her hands, as if to stave off his half-formed apology.

"I understand. I just wanted you to know I want to help you. I'm going to bring your supper here every night, and I'll have Joey haul that old cot up here so you can have a more comfortable place to sleep."

Bates looked down at his feet and shook his head. "Rhetta, you're something else," he murmured, and gazed at her with a heart-melting expression.

She heard his footsteps echo outside on the cement floor as she stood rooted to the spot. She felt as if he'd said that he loved her. "Something else," she repeated out loud.

Rhetta smiled and chided herself for feeling so pleased that she'd gained his trust. She bent down and began picking up the mountains of trash.

Rushing out the back door and down the steps, Rhetta nibbled on a cold blueberry muffin as she went. She'd overslept and would be late opening the library if she didn't hurry.

She'd stayed late at Bates's office last night, tidying up and then bringing his meal to him in the design room. It was close to one when she finally left him hard at work.

Rhetta saw Faye standing on the steps to her café like an overweight tiger lying in wait for her. Rhetta rolled her eyes heavenward and prepared herself for one of Faye's lamentations.

Wearing a purple sweater and knee socks, Faye flagged Rhetta down. "Well, what are you going to do?" Faye asked without any preamble.

"About what?" Rhetta glanced at her watch in agitation and also to give Faye a none-too-subtle hint.

"Well, you're mayor, Rhetta! You keep better informed than that, don't you?" Seeing Rhetta's blank look, Faye expelled an exaggerated sigh. "There's a bunch of people who's going over to the bank to take all 'a their money out 'cause they think it's gonna fold on account of Bates's business failing. And why you let a scoundrel like that in this town, I'll never know."

Rhetta had had enough—from everyone. "Let me tell you and your busybody friends a thing or two, Miss Kern," Rhetta said, thoroughly angry by now. "In the first place, that bank isn't about to close down, because it's part of the biggest bank in Jasper, and in the second place, Bates's business isn't about to fail. I heard it in strictest confidence that Bates is working on a million-dollar invention that'll make the people who believed in him—like Justus and Nanny— billionaires by this time next year." Rhetta knew Faye would have that tidbit spread all over town by lunchtime. "So the next time you and your cronies get together to malign somebody's business, you'd better think twice, or you'll end up looking pretty foolish a year from now." Rhetta nodded briefly at Faye's round-eyed expression and hurried down the street.

She'd never before in her life talked back to her elders like that, and she was as surprised at her outburst as Faye was. But now that it was over, she was glad. She was tired of everyone talking Bates down and saying mean things about him when his business was going through tough times.

She opened the door to the library and stepped inside. Right on her heels was Jim Hopkins, the banker.

He was a mousy-looking man with thin reddish-blond hair and pale thin lips. He looked as if he worried a lot, and Rhetta knew for a fact that he put the stereotypical stingy banker to shame. He raised being frugal to an art form.

But the man did understand how to make money. He was considered one of the best investment bankers in all of East Texas. That was why his sudden appearance worried her.

Sighing, she placed her purse and lightweight coat in the closet. As if to prepare herself, she pushed up the sleeves of her aqua sweater and turned to greet Jim Hopkins warmly. "Why, Jim, I haven't seen you since May Louise was christened three weeks ago last Sunday. How in the world are you?"

"Fine, Rhetta, fine. Do you have any coffee?" He sat down in a straight-backed chair and faced her.

"Is instant all right?"

"Sure." He crossed his legs at the knee, pulled at the crease of his navy-blue pants and waited until she returned with the coffee.

"Anything special you want to talk about, Jim?" Rhetta asked as she sat down in her swivel chair.

"Well, yes, Rhetta. We're a little worried over at the bank." He looked at her with light brown eyes that didn't blink. Rhetta kept her face blank.

"What's the matter?"

"It's Bates, Rhetta."

Rhetta swallowed and lowered her eyes, fearing that their expression might betray her.

"We've been hearing a lot of talk about how his business wasn't doing too well, but we didn't believe it. This morning, Bates called and said he needed a loan to make payroll this month. Now I know and you know that it takes time to get a business off the ground, but it also takes a special kind of person to do that." He eyed Rhetta.

"And you want to know if Bates is that special kind of person, right?" Rhetta guessed.

"Rhetta, I'm sure as hell glad that I don't have to spell things out for you." They both laughed, and then Rhetta looked down and fingered the pleats in her skirt, her expression sobering.

Reluctantly, Rhetta raised her gaze level with Jim's. "Well, you know when Bates first came here, I was dead set against him."

"I remember." Jim nodded, as if to urge her on, and his brown gaze became serious, subdued.

"I... I was very surprised when Bates stuck to that Development Committee and worked as hard as he did." She took a sip of her coffee and ran a glossy pink fingernail around her cuticle. She paused. Rhetta didn't want Bates to appear in an unfavorable light, but at the same time, as mayor of Tuckerville, it was her job to do what was best for the town.

"Rhetta?" Jim prompted when she remained silent.

"I don't know," she said flatly and met his studious gaze.

"But what do *you* think?" he prompted.

"Jim, you know Bates as well as I do, or at least, for as long as I have, and, well, you know what he was like growing up here. He's always been unpredictable. *I've* never been able to read him, at any rate." Rhetta shrugged as she struggled to get a handle on her true thoughts. "Bates is a risk taker. He seems to know the computer industry and he works constantly. We haven't seen him at the boarding house for months now," she added, gesturing with her hand. She took a deep breath and closed her eyes. "But, personally, I'd gamble on him to win just because he usually does win."

Jim shook his head and rose to his feet, then stuck his hand deep into the pocket of his trousers and jingled his change. He turned to leave.

Rhetta stood up abruptly. "Jim?" She pressed her fingertips together to form a steeple. "Are—are you going to loan him the money?" she asked in a hoarse half whisper.

Jim turned and faced her. "If it were up to me," he stated quietly, "I'd loan him the money in a minute. But I have to face the board." Jim nodded to Rhetta in lieu of a goodbye and walked out the door.

There had never been any snow in Tuckerville on Christmas Eve for as long as Rhetta could remember. Since the temperature was generally very mild in this area of East Texas, she had never even expected any. But tonight, it was chilly enough for a blazing fire.

The house was way too quiet. It seemed to creak each time a gust of wind came through. Rhetta sat in the parlor, where the Christmas tree was lit up with twinkling white lights and a gentle fire glowed on the hearth. The smell of pine boughs mingled companionably with the lingering aroma of a fresh-baked rum cake, for lunch tomorrow with Nanny and Justus and, hopefully, Bates.

All of her boarders had left to spend the holidays with relatives. Including Nanny. She was over at Justus's house, nursing him with a zeal that Justus swore would put Florence Nightingale to shame.

So Rhetta was alone, waiting, hoping Bates would come home. It was funny, though, she thought to herself as she sat staring into the glowing orange embers nestled beneath the burning logs, she really didn't know if Bates was coming or not. He hadn't said he was, and she hadn't asked, but somehow she knew he would come. And they would be all alone. Rhetta shivered and smiled to herself in anticipation.

She pulled her cream-colored shawl closer around her shoulders and went to the window. The sky was dark and cold, with a half moon looking down on all the world. Minnie Bookerton's house was all lit up with fat, multicolored lights, and Rhetta knew that right about now, Minnie would give Sir Francis Drake a bowlful of eggnog laced with brandy to lap up while she enjoyed her own cup.

Rhetta could smell her hot chocolate simmering in the kitchen and decided to go ahead and indulge before Bates came home. She was halfway to the kitchen when she heard the front door open. She turned and headed back the way she'd come.

But, even so, Bates saw her first. And he thought he'd never before felt such a fierce longing jolt through him at the mere sight of a woman. She was dressed in a long velvet skirt of forest green and a cream-colored Irish lace blouse with a high collar. A lacy cotton shawl was draped across her shoulders, and her hair, burnished to a deep amber shade by the dim lighting, was piled high on top of her head. Her face looked peaceful and serene, and there was such a welcoming warmth in her expression that he thought she might stay with him after all was said and done tonight.

He cleared his throat. "You look real pretty, Rhetta," he said quietly.

There was a subdued air about him, but such a burning intensity of desire in his eyes that Rhetta knew the night could reach but one conclusion. An answering flame deepened her eyes to passionate blue as she came toward him.

"Thank you," she murmured huskily, suddenly feeling she'd been very artful by dressing up for him. "Would you like some hot chocolate?"

"That sounds wonderful." He smiled tiredly and turned to hang up his jacket on the coatrack by the entryway.

Rhetta turned and walked into the kitchen, but he didn't follow. She got two mugs, added a small amount of brandy and a cinnamon stick to each cup and poured in the steaming hot chocolate. Rhetta stirred the cups with the cinnamon sticks and breathed in the inviting aroma.

Balancing a platter of Christmas cookies in one hand and holding the mugs of hot chocolate in the other, she made her way from the kitchen and into the parlor to find Bates nearly nodding off in the reclining chair.

"Are visions of sugarplums dancing in your head?" she teased lightly. As she placed the cookies and hot chocolate on the coffee table in front of the fire, Bates slid out of the chair to the floor and rested his back against the recliner. "Come here." He tilted his head back and, with narrowed eyes, beckoned to her.

Rhetta felt her stomach flip over and her breath lodge somewhere in her chest. She had never before had a man look at her quite like that. It was pleasantly unnerving. Feeling her heartbeat quicken, Rhetta floated around the coffee table to kneel on the floor beside him.

Slowly he reached up and, one by one, gently tugged the pins from her hair until the auburn tresses toppled down around her shoulders in loose curls. He pulled her across him and crushed her lips to his in a fierce, demanding kiss that branded her as his for life.

Then the kiss mellowed, and he rubbed his lips gently against hers, tantalizing her with his nearness yet never giving her full satisfaction. Rhetta moaned hungrily and pressed herself more fully against his chest.

"My God, Rhetta, you haunt me," he said hoarsely. He kissed her again and again, driving her closer and closer to the edge with complete mastery. Her nails bit into his shoulders, and she closed her eyes tightly, feeling his tongue slide slowly into her mouth and then letting her tongue follow his back. Letting her lips slide slowly down to her jawline, he traced a line of shimmering, icy-hot fire down her neck until Rhetta's senses were pitched to a feverish arousal.

Sliding his hand down her chest, he cupped her breast, feeling it swell to spill from his palm. Bates took a trembling breath and slid his hand lower....

Rhetta pulled her head up shakily and looked into his eyes, begging, wanting, hoping.

Bates could read the message in her eyes and he bit his lower lip in concentration. *She'll hate me, if I tell her afterwards. Tell her now, you coward.*

He took a deep breath, and Rhetta looked away. She knew the moment was gone.

"Do you want some hot chocolate, Bates?" You already asked him that, stupid, she thought in irritation.

Rhetta reached for the two mugs and handed one to him without waiting for his answer.

"Thanks." They sipped their drinks silently, staring into the red-hot embers. Bates got up, poked the fire to life and added another log, which crackled and popped as the flames licked over it. He moved the coffee table over to the side so that they could lean back against the recliner and have an unobstructed view of the fire. He sat back down beside Rhetta and pulled her close against him. Rhetta snuggled up against his hard body and felt bewildered.

What was the matter with him? And what was the matter with her? She acted like a wanton around him. And he had turned her down again. She didn't understand his actions. She'd shown him that she wanted him and was on his side about his business.

"Rhetta?" His deep, resonant baritone broke the heavy silence.

Rhetta's frustrations burst out all at once. "Why don't you want to make love to me?" she asked angrily. She swung her head around to face him, her eyes mirroring all the ache and hurt that had been bottled up inside.

Bates expelled a short breath, looked into the fire and then back at Rhetta's bewildered face. "Look at you," he said, taking in her old-fashioned blouse and long velveteen skirt. "Rhetta, did it ever occur to you that I'm paying you a very high compliment by not taking you to bed?"

"No," she said flatly. "I don't know how you could be paying me a compliment when you're rejecting me." Rhetta pressed the fleshy part of her thumb into the velveteen material of her skirt and wiggled her thumb back and forth.

Bates ran his fingers through his hair, rumpling it even more. "Rhetta, what I'm trying to say is this— you aren't that kind of girl."

"Yes I am!" Rhetta rushed on: "I want to be."

"Rhetta," Bates said, smiling indulgently, "I can't let you do this. I may not be here tomorrow. My company may not make it over the next couple of months, and then I'd have to leave. I couldn't stay in Tuckerville. Surely you see that?''

Rhetta bowed her head and nodded.

"And you really aren't the kind of girl for a one-night stand, are you?''

When he put it like that, she'd sound like a floozy if she said, "Yes, I want to have a one-night stand. No strings attached, pal. What did you say your name was?'' So Rhetta said, "No, I wouldn't want a one-night stand, Bates."

"That's what I thought,'' he said, a resigned note entering his voice. He hadn't been around a really old-fashioned girl since he was a teenager. And he knew he wasn't a teenager any longer. It was a strange sensation for him to pull back when he wanted to dive deeper and deeper.

But he was past the immature stage of taking what he wanted just because he wanted it. He cared about Rhetta, and he wanted what was best for her in the long run, not a momentary burst of pleasure. Bates ground his teeth together at that last thought.

Rhetta sat up straighter. "I have something for you." She rushed over to the Christmas tree and retrieved a package. "It's for you,'' she said, suddenly shy.

Bates took the package from her and opened it. It was a one-year medallion with "McCabe Enterprises, Inc." engraved on the back.

"It's a little early, but it's just to show you that I have faith in you.''

Bates sighed. "I thought I'd be able to put this off, but I can't since you gave me this gift. Um, I'm filing for bankruptcy in February if this big contract I'm working on doesn't come through. Right now, it doesn't appear that I'll be able to complete my invention in time." He issued the statements in a flat, clipped voice that held a wealth of bitterness.

"Oh, Bates." She put her hand on his arm and squeezed. "I'm so sorry." She shook her head in dismay and wondered if he would leave immediately.

"Rhetta?"

Rhetta looked at him.

"I have something for you, too," he said sheepishly, rubbing his hand across his five-o'clock shadow as if he was contemplating whether to give his present to her. "To tell the truth, I didn't remember it was Christmas Eve until after six o'clock, and by then all the stores were closed. So that's why I was so late. I finally found this." He removed an envelope from his shirt pocket.

Rhetta took it from his fingers. On the front was a scarecrow with pumpkins all around it. The caption read, Happy Halloween! And below, Bates had written, "Rhetta, Merry Christmas to someone who was there when I really needed her." There was a small dash and then he'd signed it simply, "Bates." Rhetta looked up at him, puzzled.

Bates stared back at her for a minute. "I bought that for you on Halloween and never had the chance to give it to you. I bought you a cupcake, too, but I ate that."

A bubble of laughter escaped her lips. "Well, I guess I'll never be able to say that you're unoriginal."

He gave her a wry grin, then rolled over and laid his head down in her lap, looking up at her face, which was softened by the fire's glow. Rhetta smoothed the hair back from his brow and kissed his eyelids shut. Running her fingers through his hair, she contemplated their future.

She'd always drawn parallels between their relationship and his computer business and now wondered if, like his computer business, their relationship would fizzle out. Rhetta knew now that she loved him, loved every stubborn, willful bone in his body. She loved the whole man. She looked down at his stubborn features. Even in repose his chin was thrust out at an aggressive angle. His deep, even breathing clued Rhetta to the fact that he was fast asleep.

Rhetta thought back over her childhood crush on him and their first moments on the porch last summer, then looked down at him.

This was the man. The man she had fought against from the beginning, because even then she'd known that once Bates McCabe had captured her heart, he would never release it.

Chapter Nine

Bates glanced at himself in a shop window as he strode briskly down the street on his way to the bank. His chin was thrust out so far that he looked belligerent. Well, hell, he felt belligerent.

He opened the door to the bank and walked in. Ignoring all the curious stares from the tellers and bank customers, he walked straight past the secretaries and the desks of minor bank officers and straight into Jim Hopkins's office. "What in the hell is this all about?" he demanded, tossing the request for his financial statement and for his presence at a bank board meeting this morning on Jim's desk.

Instantly Jim Hopkins rose to his feet with a welcoming smile on his face, as if he were greeting his best friend. "Bates! Good to see you." He walked around his oversize mahogany desk and slapped Bates on the back in greeting.

Bates gave him an icy stare. "I want to know what this meeting is all about."

"Now, Bates," Jim said in a placating tone, "it's customary in every bank to ask for year-end financial statements from all large loan customers. You are no exception to that rule."

"I'm very familiar with banking practices, Jim, and I still want to know what this meeting is all about. We had an agreement, damn it." Bates banged his fist down on the desk and coffee sloshed out of Jim's cup and onto some papers.

"Why don't we sit down and discuss this rationally, Bates." Jim gestured to the two black leather chairs in front of his desk and his mouth thinned into a straight line.

"Because I don't feel rational, by God." Bates paced up and down the large oriental rug like a caged bull.

"Now I know you're upset, Bates, but look at it from our point of view. We've got a lot of money invested in you, and we just need to know we're going to get it back."

Bates stopped pacing and turned to look at Jim. "You never will get it back if you don't let me get back to work. I'm on the verge of closing a big contract this week, if I can produce enough units. And now you're calling me down to the bank to discuss my loans. This bank's self-destructive. You're self-destructive!" he bellowed.

"Bates, I'm not the only member on this board." He looked frankly at Bates.

Bates paused heavily and sighed. "Oh, Lord, let's get it over with." He rubbed the back of his neck with his hand and took a deep breath, trying to calm himself. They *could* call his loan if he told them what he really thought about their damned bank meetings.

They walked down a dark hallway with carpeting so thick that Bates's feet seemed to sink half an inch. Then Jim ushered him into the boardroom, which was intimidating with its overstated plush furnishings.

Bates took the bull by the horns. He sat down at the head of the table in a high-backed maroon leather chair. Jim grinned, and whispered, "I like a man with guts."

When everyone was seated, Bates stated in a voice that was more a growl than anything else, "What do you want to know about *my* business?"

Several board members cleared their throats and a couple loosened their ties, but Jim Hopkins couldn't keep the grin off his face. "I think, Bates, they want to know why your business couldn't make payroll last month."

"I'll tell you why." Bates leaned forward, and looked them each in turn in the eyes as he spoke. "Around the first of November I delivered on a contract with a computer-supply company that filed for bankruptcy in December. So I didn't get paid. I may never get paid,'' he stated simply and sat back in his chair.

"Well, Mr. McCabe,'' said Mrs. Simmons, whose wealthy status was the direct result of marrying three elderly gentlemen, "that's all well and good, but you should allow for little contingencies like that.'' She shook a fat finger weighted down by a vulgarly large sapphire at him. "It's not good—''

"Look, Mrs. Simmons,'' he interrupted, casting an uninterested glance at the three inches of cleavage she displayed, "I'm no fortune teller. I don't have a crystal ball where I can see into the future, and neither do you,'' he added pointedly. "No business makes money its first year in operation, and I've had plenty of extenuating circumstances.'' The board members squirmed uncomfortably under his piercing scrutiny. "You've barely given me enough time to set things up, and already you're sticking your nose in and preventing me from doing what I'm supposed to be doing. What I'm best at doing.'' He rose abruptly to his feet and all eyes followed him. "Ladies and gentlemen, let's not waste any more time.''

"All right then, Bates. We'll lay it on the line,'' Jim said easily. "The next time you can't make payroll, we'll call the loans and force you into bankruptcy.'' He paused to let the gravity of his words sink in, then smiled, the gap between his teeth making his appearance more menacing. "Fair enough?''

Bates looked hard at Jim, wanting to call him every name in the book for reneging on a promise. But he didn't. He wanted their loan money. "Fair enough,'' he bit out. He tapped his fingers on the table in a contemptuous, dismissive manner, pivoted as sharply as a dancer and strode purposefully out the double doors.

"Bates, please. Let's just go down there and see what they have to say," Rhetta pleaded.

"Rhetta, I know what they have to say. They're a bunch of jackasses. They want to run my company. To hell with them." Bates paced the floor of his office, hands stuffed in his pockets and a deep scowl on his face.

"Bates. You have to go. They'll recall your loans."

"Let them," he shot back. "I don't give a damn."

Rhetta sat forward in his office chair, leaned her elbows on his desk and rubbed her temples. "Bates, it will get back to Justus and he'll be upset. And he doesn't need to be any more upset." *Had she really stooped that low? Emotional blackmail?*

Bates looked stricken. Even though everyone had assured him that Justus had no idea that the business was in trouble, Bates still blamed himself. He suspected that anxiety had been the cause of the older man's heart attack. "Maybe you're right." Bates looked so tired and guilty that Rhetta felt like a heel for tricking him into going.

But on the other hand, if he didn't go, the bankers *would* recall his loans, with no questions asked.

Rhetta knew that Bates was walking on the edge. He'd gone too many months with too little sleep and too many pressures to take much more.

"Listen, Bates, we can just go down there and tell them that things are looking up and that in two months you'll give them a better report, and then we'll leave."

"What do you mean 'we'?" He stopped pacing and looked at Rhetta.

"We. You and me," Rhetta explained patiently, smoothing down the bulky collar of her black turtleneck sweater dress.

"Rhetta, no. You don't want to get yourself mixed up with me. If I have to leave Tuckerville, I don't want to ruin the rest of your life here. They'll blame you. For years, they'll blame you."

Then take me with you.

She'll never leave Tuckerville. It's so much a part of her now.

Rhetta looked down at his desk and then calmly back up at him. "I'm going with you, Bates," she stated quietly. Picking up her purse and coat, she walked toward the door. "Coming?" She looked back at him, determined.

Bates read her look accurately, grinned and grabbed his briefcase before following her out the door.

Once inside the bank, Bates slipped his arm around her shoulders and said, "We make quite a team, Rhetta Tucker."

Rhetta flushed and felt as if she'd just been handed the moon on a silver platter. "Let's hope the bankers think so," Rhetta murmured as they were ushered into the rich interior of the boardroom.

This time, Bates noticed, the maroon leather chairs at either end of the table were both occupied, and Jim Hopkins was not smiling.

The heavy beige curtains were drawn so that not even a sliver of welcoming sunlight peeked through. All around the boardroom, stern faces stared at Bates and Rhetta. Bates squared his jaw and pulled his shoulders back, like a soldier ready to do battle.

"Rhetta, Bates, please have a seat," Jim said quietly as he gestured to two empty chairs.

Bates's expression became harder, but Rhetta reacted to Jim's serious manner with shaking knees.

"Bates, we've called this meeting because we're more than worried. We've just received word that you've been cutting hours among some of your employees. Is this true?"

"Of course, it's true, Jim. That's how I was able to meet payroll and my expenses this month," Bates said tersely.

"What exactly are you planning to do about this situation?" Jim asked politely.

"I followed your rules—I didn't borrow more money to meet payroll." He leaned forward across the table, as if preparing to lunge at Jim at any minute. "The rest is none of your damned business," Bates snapped.

"I'm afraid it is, Bates." Jim sat back in his chair, his manner relaxed and easy, as if he were discussing building a lemonade stand with his children. "You see, we've invested a pretty hefty chunk of our assets in your company's future, and when we see your company looking shaky, well, we need to know what the problem is.''

"Until I go bankrupt, you can just keep out of my company. I'm running it just fine and I'll let you know when I'm in trouble. Otherwise, just keep out." Bates rose to his feet, ignoring Rhetta's hand as she tried to keep him seated.

"Jim, please don't recall his loan." Rhetta turned the full force of her blue eyes on Jim. "I'll put up my house and inheritance as collateral—"

"Rhetta," Bates commanded in a clipped voice, "be quiet!" He turned to Jim Hopkins, his expression flinty. "Jim, my terms still stand." He nodded briefly to Jim, turned and left the meeting without a backward glance at Rhetta.

Rhetta stayed where she was, glued to her chair, listening to the heavy doors slowly close. She looked pleadingly at Jim, who nodded at her.

"Will it satisfy you all if Rhetta puts her home and inheritance up as collateral to extend Bates's loan for a few more months?"

Rhetta didn't even check to see if the other board members had agreed to it. She stood up and left the room, knowing that she had just announced to the town of Tuckerville that she was in love with Bates McCabe.

"I hardly know what I'm doing," Nanny exclaimed as Rhetta looked on indulgently.

"Well, it's not every day you get married, Nanny Fields." Rhetta smoothed the back of Nanny's navy blue linen suit and smiled with affection at Nanny's uncharacteristic nervousness.

"I thank the good Lord above for that bit of fortune," Nanny muttered dryly as she patted her hair into place for the third time in five minutes. She turned panic-stricken eyes to Rhetta. "You don't think this is silly, do you?" she asked. "I mean, getting married after all these years?"

"Of course not," Rhetta said, dismissing the older woman's anxieties easily. "Nanny, if you leave Justus standing at the altar he'll kill you. Now, you look beautiful. You're supposed to be nervous and have second thoughts, Nanny. It's your first marriage and—"

"But you don't think I look ridiculous or anything, like those tacky old women who try to look sixteen when everyone knows they're fifty if they're a day?"

Rhetta swallowed the bubble of laughter that rose in her throat and tried to calm Nanny's last-minute jitters. "Of course not, now put this garter belt on."

"Oh, Lord, I'm glad you reminded me." Nanny modestly turned her back to Rhetta and slid the "something borrowed" up her spindly leg. "I hope it stays up."

"Step back and let me look at you." Rhetta eyed her thoughtfully, tilting her head to the side, trying to figure out what was missing. She snapped her fingers. "We forgot your veil."

"You mean my mask," Nanny mocked. "I'm just afraid Justus will turn and run when he lifts up that veil and sees how old I look." Nanny picked up the navy blue hat with the short netted veil and Rhetta helped her secure it to her tightly curled hair. She stepped back again to survey Nanny's appearance, then nodded in satisfaction.

"All right now, I'll go get George to take some pictures of you in the bridal suite."

"Bridal suite? This is my bedroom!"

"I know Nanny, now just calm down. You aren't spending the night here, I just called it that 'cause you're getting dressed in here."

"Oh," Nanny said, and laughed a little at her panicky reactions.

Rhetta returned a few minutes later with George the plumber, who was also the local photographer.

"All right, ladies, stand over there together by the dressing table. The bride and her maid of honor."

Rhetta stood beside Nanny, her pale peach, calf-length bridesmaid dress a perfect foil to her amber hair, falling loosely at her shoulders. As she scooted closer to Nanny, she hugged her and couldn't help thinking that Nanny and Justus should have married long ago.

George snapped their picture, and Rhetta hugged Nanny to her side and then stepped to the side, for the next picture of Nanny.

"Now, Nanny," George said, "why don't you lift your dress a little so we can get a picture of the garter."

"I will not!" Nanny said indignantly. "Land sakes, have you lost your mind!" she cried out huffily, drawing back as if he might attack her.

Rhetta intervened before Nanny could bonk him over the head with a book or poke him with her hat pin. "Now, Nanny," she said soothingly, "that's a very traditional picture, to have the bride showing the garter. Everyone does it."

Nanny eyed her skeptically. Then she turned her back to both of them. She turned back around. "I'm ready." She lifted her skirt a scant three inches above her ankle to where she had slid the garter belt down to a more respectable level.

George rolled his eyes and Rhetta smothered a smile at Nanny's prudish behavior.

There was a series of rapid knocks on the door. "Nanny, hurry up in there. Justus is going to start the wedding without you," Bates teased.

Rhetta's heart started beating wildly. She couldn't wait to see Bates. He'd been gone for about a week.

"You go on over there, Bates. Rhetta and I will be over shortly." Nanny waited until she heard his footsteps go down the hall and then she shooed George out of the room. Rhetta and Nanny were alone again.

Nanny took a deep breath as she looked around her simple room and then at Rhetta. "Guess I won't be coming back here anymore," she said, her voice wobbly. She ran a finger over the curving lines of the bedpost. Her wrinkled lips curved into a reminiscent smile. "I was twenty-two when I first came to live in this room." She looked over at the faded flowered wallpaper, her blue eyes watery. "That was before you were born, before Bates came here, too. I thought I'd died and gone to heaven when the court gave me custody of Bates after my sister died." She looked out the window into T. Johnson's tidy backyard, shook her head and pursed her lips together, her eyelids batting rapidly. "I couldn't have kids. I knew that. And even when Justus swore it didn't matter, I wouldn't marry him. A man ought to have a son. Justus should have married long ago."

"Oh, Nanny," Rhetta said tearfully. "He's always loved you."

Nanny looked over at her. "I know. I know that now. It was my stupid pride that said I wasn't a whole woman and that no one would ever want a woman who couldn't have kids." She pulled herself together and wiped away the tears beneath her eyes. "Now I think that's about the silliest thing I've ever done." She paused and fingered the fabric of her skirt. "It's funny how time changes things like that."

Rhetta smiled softly, her throat aching with suppressed emotion. She leaned forward and tenderly kissed Nanny's soft, wrinkled cheek.

Nanny sniffed and turned her head away sharply. "We'd better git, or Justus will think I'm not coming!"

Once at Justus's house, Nanny sent an order for Justus to go into the back room so he wouldn't see her until the ceremony.

Rhetta walked into the living room, where the service was to be held. The minister was there, going over his notes, but her gaze went instantly to the tall man with dark curling hair who had stolen her heart.

"Hello, Rhetta," he said softly.

Rhetta could have sworn that his whole body leaned forward when she walked into the room. He was as eager to see her as she was to see him. A dark light lit up his blue eyes and Rhetta stood frozen, unable to move.

He was so handsome that Rhetta's hungry gaze drank in the sight of him. The navy-blue suit deepened his naturally swarthy complexion and emphasized his broad shoulders, lean hips and long legs, making him seem larger than life. His chest rose and fell visibly with each breath, and his dark blue eyes seemed to penetrate her soul as he looked over at her. The hollows beneath his cheeks only served to make him look leaner and more attractive. He'd lost weight, but that hadn't affected the breadth of his shoulders, which seemed to loom up like a bear's as he came toward her and kissed her cheek.

Rhetta inhaled his familiar male scent and wanted to sway into his broad chest and lay her head against him. *Dear Lord, would this torment never end? Could he ever love me?* Rhetta shook her head in answer to her own silent question.

The chords from a familiar classic filled the room as the pianist from the church began playing the piece from Bach that Justus had selected to precede Nanny's entry with the traditional bridal march.

Rhetta and Bates took their places across from each other. Justus beamed at Rhetta, looking healthier and happier than she'd seen him since long before his heart attack. He was resplendent in a black suit and a gray, black and white striped tie. He winked at Rhetta and she winked back.

Nanny and Justus had decided, since Justus had no family living, to have Rhetta as the maid of honor and Bates as the best man and have no other guests.

The pianist played the first three notes of the bridal march, and Nanny peeped around the corner. Rhetta grinned and Justus caught his breath at the sight of the woman he'd waited to marry for forty years.

Nanny walked regally into the living room, skirt rustling. She stopped beside Justus and slipped her arm through his, patting his hand. Their eyes met in the fulfillment of a union that had been started long ago.

The minister cleared his throat and began the familiar words, making Rhetta's heart ache with longing.

She wanted to be married. To Bates. She looked over at him. His strong features were touched with unaccustomed gentleness as he looked at the two people who had practically been his mother and father.

Rhetta swallowed as tears welled up in her eyes as she thought about the days ahead. They were numbered. Bates had told her at Christmas that this business couldn't last through February if things didn't pick up, and Rhetta hadn't seen any sign of that yet.

Today was February fourteenth, Valentine's Day. Nanny and Justus's wedding day. Rhetta blinked back the tears in her eyes and stared unseeing as Nanny and Justus repeated their vows, their voices tender and hushed with the import of the moment.

She knew this was probably also goodbye to Bates. He could never stay in Tuckerville if his business were to fail, because the town was too much against him. Rhetta sighed. She knew in her heart that if he asked her, she'd even leave the one thing most dear to her: Tuckerville.

But he wouldn't. She couldn't change him just because she'd been stupid enough to fall in love with a man who preferred travel and risk to marriage and family. No, you couldn't change people.

Bates looked over the gray heads of his aunt Nanny and Justus at Rhetta. And all that he could see were her eyes. Her eyes haunted him with their quiet certainty. He'd struggled to escape but couldn't. He wanted her. God, he wanted her.

The only thing that had saved him from taking her was his failing business. And his protective feeling for her.

He'd never experienced that before. He'd never wanted to shelter a woman before. Protect her from himself. Rhetta brought out in him all of those things that people say are very sentimental, gentle things. He wanted to cherish her, make things easier for her. He shifted his feet uncomfortably.

He knew she was wondering what in the world was the matter with him. Why he hadn't tried to see her more when he responded so readily to her physically. But he knew that if he made love to Rhetta, he'd lose himself in her and want to drown himself in her. Forever.

He wanted not just one night or a thousand nights, but to wake up with her when she was fifty and had wrinkles.

The fear that he would lose her was a reality now. She was going away from him. She was so womanly. So much a woman. A lady. A real lady.

But he couldn't expect a woman like her to share the agony of building a business. Though he also knew that she would if he asked her.

But Bates couldn't bring himself to allow her to do anything for him. He knew he'd marry her tomorrow if his business was going strong, but marriage now would be unfair. It would tie her to a man who had a strong possibility of going bankrupt, of failing in the next two weeks. No, he couldn't do that to her.

He'd have to leave Tuckerville if his business failed. They'd kick him out of town and Rhetta wouldn't be able to stand leaving. She loved Tuckerville. She'd fought hard for it, and he couldn't take her heritage away from her. Not if he really loved her.

Chapter Ten

Already Minnie Bookerton's tulips were popping up, and it wasn't even mid-March, although the weather today was seventy-two degrees.

Rhetta was outside, working the soil around her oak tree, preparing it for the caladiums she would plant around the base of the tree when the weather steadied out to a consistently warm temperature. She stood up, tugging at her shorts, which had bunched up too high as she was gardening, and enjoying the coolness of the moist dirt beneath her bare feet.

Stretching, Rhetta squinted up at the sun through the branches of the tree and caught sight of a cardinal darting in among the new leaves, which were just beginning to unfurl.

"Hey, beautiful."

Rhetta turned around slowly, knowing there was only one voice that could make her heart beat faster just by uttering a sound. "Hello, Bates," she said softly. "What are you doing home so early on a Friday afternoon?"

Her glance ran over him in quick appraisal. He was still wearing his suit, but he had slung his jacket over his shoulder, and his pale blue shirt was rolled up at the sleeves to expose his muscular forearms. Navy-blue slacks accentuated the length of his legs, and there was a careless grin on his face. Rhetta shifted her gaze back down to the soil and wiggled her toes into the coolness of it.

Bates walked up to her and placed his arms across her shoulders so that his jacket draped down her back. She could smell the faint scent of soap from his morning shower still clinging to him—no perfumed after-shave for him, just good clean soap.

She looked up into his eyes and then rubbed her cheek against his arm, much like a cat. The hair on his arm tickled her skin.

He watched as the cool spring breeze lifted a strand of her auburn hair up from her shoulders and dropped it back down again. "I've got some good news." He stroked his thumb across her cheekbone. "Last week I was able to deliver on that big contract, and today we got paid for it. They also accepted my bid on another deal, which we should get paid for in a week. So—" he took a deep breath and paused "—it looks like we'll break even."

"That's wonderful!" Rhetta hugged him to her, a tide of warmth seeping through as she pressed her body against the hardness of his. He slid his hand down her back and under the cotton material of her thin shirt. Rhetta shivered uncontrollably with longing.

"Mmmm, so's this." He nuzzled her neck, and the fine hair along her nape stood up at attention.

Rhetta arched her body to the side, allowing him better access to the sensitive skin of her throat. "And how's the invention coming?" she murmured.

"Oh, that feels good," he said as she began massaging the muscles at the back of his neck. "Late last night I put the finishing touches on my invention."

"Oh, I'm sorry, Bates," she exclaimed suddenly and pulled back.

"What's the matter?"

"I got some mud on your collar from the garden." Wiping the small amount of mud off her fingers, she put her hands on her hips and cocked her head to one side. "Did you say you've finished your invention?"

"Yes," he said slowly, watching her steadily.

"Why, that's wonderful! We should go see Nanny and Justus and celebrate!"

"Whoa, there," he said, laughing. "We have to sell it next. I've got an appointment next Thursday with the biggest computer-supply company in the southwest. I want you to come with me. To Houston."

Rhetta caught her breath. She knew it didn't mean anything, but this was the first time in a long while that he'd asked her to do anything with him. "I'd love to go," she said softly, curling her hair behind her ear. "I can probably get Ruth Lee to do the cooking while I'm gone. The twins hate her cooking," she added with a twinge of guilt.

"Then they'll appreciate you more." Bates grinned.

"Speaking of which, I've got to go in and start supper or it'll never be ready in time." Rhetta moved out of his arms reluctantly.

"Are you going to be around after dinner tonight?" He rubbed his knuckles across his chin.

"Yes," she answered, and waited expectantly for him to ask her out.

"Good." Bates turned and walked up the back porch steps ahead of her, whistling as he went.

Rhetta sat down on the white wicker rocker where Nanny used to sit and sighed forlornly. She couldn't understand it. She'd thought Bates would come to see her tonight, but right after dinner he'd bolted away, and then she'd heard the roar of his car engine.

Dinner conversation had been full of Bates's business and how well he was doing. Reverend McFarland had included Bates in the blessing by thanking God for bringing prosperity to Tuckerville, and Joey Heckenkemper had extended his hand in congratulations to Bates. Miss Ruth Lee had winked at Bates and tweaked Rhetta's cheek, certain they'd announce a wedding any day now.

Now there was an uneasy feeling growing in Rhetta's stomach, and she couldn't quite fathom why she wasn't as excited as she should be about Bates's business success. Perhaps it was because she liked helping him, and he wouldn't need her any longer.

But her sense of apprehension held something more. There was something she was afraid of, something that scared her as much as the fear that his business would fail and he would have to leave Tuckerville.

Rhetta looked up at the sky. Thousands of tiny stars were scattered in varying formations across the heavens, and there was a hazy moon that was three-quarters full.

Car lights flashed down the street, and Rhetta's heart lurched suddenly. The black car stopped in front of the boarding house, and a car door slammed shut.

Rhetta made a motion to get up from her chair and then stopped. She didn't want Bates to think she'd been waiting for him on the front porch like an old mother hen, but it would look funny if she left now.

His steps sounded on the three steps up to the porch, and Rhetta stayed as still as a cat, watching.

"I thought you might be out here," he said casually, not at all startled by her presence.

Rhetta regarded him in silence.

"That new ice-cream parlor's opening up tonight. Do you want to walk down and get some?" he invited.

Rhetta shrugged and tried not to look too eager. "Sure, let me get my shoes." She pushed herself out of the rocker and stood. The rocker creaked back and forth over the gray floorboards.

Bates rested his back against a porch column and crossed his arms over his chest. "In all the years I've known you, you have never had your shoes on except when you've been going into town," Bates said with affection.

"I don't like them," she replied as she hurried into the kitchen to grab her shoes from underneath the chopping table.

"Ready," she called as she stepped out the door and onto the front porch. She leaned over to slip her sandals on her feet, and Bates moved near her and caught her arm to steady her. A lightning flash of awareness shot through her at his touch. Rhetta straightened quickly, and Bates took her hand and led her down the porch steps.

There was a spring in her step as she walked beside him, but she tried to contain her excitement at being with him.

It was silly. She always felt so young and inexperienced when she was with him. But there weren't any men like Bates in Tuckerville or any of the surrounding towns. Bates wasn't like any man she'd ever known.

"How was your day today?" His fingers caressed the soft skin on the back of her hand, his larger hand engulfing her smaller one.

"Fine. A man from a car-manufacturing company came with Senator Hawkins to look over Tuckerville as a site for a new plant. There are about three more sites they're looking at—in Tennessee, Oklahoma and, I think, Arkansas." Rhetta skirted a big hole in the sidewalk where the recent spring rains had made a puddle of muddy water.

"Hmm. That sounds promising." Bates pulled her close to him, and their arms pressed against each other as they walked. He looked up at the sky and shoved his free hand deep in his pocket. "I went over to see Steven Sutphen today and noticed they're starting a new housing development over there."

"Oh, yes, they started the plans for that way back in December. Didn't you hear about it?" Rhetta looked at him in amazement.

"No," he answered, his mouth quirking upward in a self-deprecating grin. "If you'll remember, I've been up to my ears in work for the past year. And by the way, who was that middle-aged woman at the dinner table tonight? Is she just an overnight guest?" A dog trotted by them in the night, dog tags jingling pleasantly in the silence.

"Heavens!" Rhetta exclaimed as they crossed the street. "Haven't you had dinner with us since she came?"

"Rhetta, I haven't been home in time to eat your wonderful cooking for the past six months."

Home. That sounded so wonderful to her. Their home. "Six months?" she asked, aloud.

"Six months," he repeated firmly.

Ahead of them a cricket started chirping, and a few seconds later another joined in. They quieted again as Rhetta and Bates passed by.

"I hadn't realized it had been so long," she said slowly. "Anyway, that's Nancy Henderson. She moved here from Baton Rouge. She's my part-time secretary down at the courthouse and also keeps the library open in the afternoons.''

· "Hmm. I see you're moving up in the world." Bates arched an eyebrow at her.

"My heavens, look up ahead." Amazed, Rhetta pointed at the bright neon light flashing on and off. Tuckerville hadn't had any neon lights before. "I haven't seen that many people out together since Eustus Blakely died last January. What is it?"

"That's the new ice-cream parlor's grand opening. They're giving out free balloons." Bates watched her expression closely.

As they moved closer to the small crowd, Rhetta scanned the faces for a familiar one. "This is terrible. There's only two people I know in that whole crowd." She nodded at the familiar faces as she and Bates approached the outskirts of the group.

Bates shrugged. "That's progress. Tuckerville is growing up, Rhetta."

Rhetta scowled at all the unfamiliar faces. She didn't like not knowing who was who in Tuckerville.

"Come on, I've got an idea." He took her by the elbow and led her down the street to T. Johnson's Fountain and Druggery.

The bell attached to the doorway tinkled in the quiet store. "Hey, T," Bates called to the plump man behind the fountain, who had his chin cupped in his hand, and was bent over reading the newspaper laid flat on top of the counter. "Can you get us two of your best Coke floats?" Bates slid onto a red twirly counter seat and Rhetta followed suit, sitting beside him.

T. Johnson peered at them over his glasses and slowly lifted himself off the counter. "Thought you two would probably join ever'body else over at that fancy new ice-cream parlor." He waddled over to the soft-serve ice-cream machine and pulled down two glasses from the shelf in front of the mirror.

Bates nudged Rhetta in the ribs. "Oh, no, T. Johnson. I was just telling Rhetta the other day that there wasn't a single place in Texas that could top T. Johnson's Coke floats."

In the mirror, Rhetta could see T. Johnson smile as he swirled the ice cream into the glasses, leaving just the right amount of room for the cola to go in. He filled them to the rim with Coke, letting the creamy foam die down as much as possible before slipping two red-and-white striped straws down the center.

"That's right, Mr. Johnson. Nobody's Coke floats taste as good as yours," Rhetta said, backing Bates up in his compliments as T. Johnson set the Coke floats in front of them.

"Well, I guess the newness of that new ice-cream parlor will wear down eventually. Then my regulars will start coming in again." He nodded with satisfaction as Rhetta sipped and then stirred her float around with her straw.

"Oh, sure, T. Remember when I was working here and Mick started selling hamburgers out of his kitchen? After a week or two, all your regulars started coming back in." Bates picked up his spoon and ate the ice cream that wouldn't fit through his straw.

"Yeah." T. Johnson leaned heavily on the counter and watched them enjoying their refreshments. "Hey, Bates, I heard there's talk about namin' a street after you. How about that? From my counter boy to a big shot."

"I found that rather ironic, considering that one month ago they were talking about kicking me out of town and bankrupting me." Bates grinned wryly.

"Yes, last month you were the betrayer and this month you're the savior. Tuckerville's hearts are very fickle," Rhetta said, twirling on her red seat.

"Yeah," he agreed, "and guess who was leading the parade in both cases?" His eyebrows arched and he looked inquiringly at Rhetta's profile.

"I don't have to guess." She shook her head and her eyes shone. "Faye Kern is the only woman I know who isn't embarrassed or intimidated by anything or anyone. She has no shame."

The bell tinkled over the door, and Nanny and Justus walked in.

"Well, I'll be," T. Johnson said, "I haven't seen you since the day before you had your heart attack. And by golly, you're looking better than ever."

Justus beamed as he escorted Nanny over to a booth. "Hello, everybody. Rhetta, Bates." Justus jerked his head to call them over. "Come on over here and join us." He helped Nanny into a booth and eased himself down beside her.

"Old fool! Can't you see they want to be alone?"
Nanny admonished in a hushed tone that carried all
over the store.

Rhetta and Bates looked at each other, grinned and
twirled around simultaneously to face Nanny and
Justus. Then they slid off their stools, picked up their
floats and joined the older couple in the booth.

"Now, Aunt Nanny," Bates said, teasingly, "we
know you and Justus wanted to be alone and smooch.
You just didn't want us watching. Afraid we might
learn something."

"Don't you be giving me that hogwash, Bates
McCabe. I couldn't teach you a darn thing. With what
you know about women, you could write a whole
book. Don't you think so, Rhetta?" Nanny asked in-
nocently.

"I'm not going to touch that one." Rhetta shook
her head, smiling, and then stirred her float around
with her straw, keeping her eyes downcast.

"Well, son, I hear you hit the jackpot today," Justus said, deftly shifting the conversation.

"Well, I got paid for one of my deliveries, if that's
what you mean." Pushing his empty glass to one side,
Bates stretched his long legs into the aisle and put his
arm around Rhetta's shoulders. "The most significant thing that happened is that I put the finishing
touches on my invention late last night."

"So tonight he's on vacation," Rhetta added dryly
under her breath.

"Well, hot damn!" Justus exclaimed, ignoring
Rhetta's comment. "We ought to be millionaires by

this time next year, Nanny." He swung his brown eyes over to Bates. "When's the first royalty check due out?"

Bates laughed good-naturedly. "I'm going to tell you the same thing you told me about a month ago. Don't count your chickens before they're hatched."

"Ha ha!" Justus hooted. "Looky there, Nanny, he's gettin' too big for his britches already."

"He's always been too big for his britches, as far as I'm concerned," Nanny said wryly, and then reached over to pat Bates's free hand.

Bates drew little circles with his thumb on Rhetta's bare shoulder, creating a warm, swirling sensation in Rhetta's stomach. She wanted to be alone with Bates and have him bury his lips in her hair and smother her face with warm kisses, but his next words put an end to that dream.

"I've got to get back down to the office tonight. I told Hank I'd meet him there at ten to go over the marketing plan for the invention." Bates stood up and pulled Rhetta out of the booth with him. "Come on, Rhetta, I've got to walk you home." He took her hand and pulled her through the store.

Just as they reached the door, Justus called out, "Don't forget to kiss her good-night!"

Bates paused at the door and turned to look at Justus. "Now Justus, you know me better than that!" The little bell tinkled over their heads as they walked out into the street.

* * *

"Please."

Rhetta eyed him thoughtfully over the hood of the car. "Only if you let me win," she said.

Bates grinned and shook his head. "Can't do it. Losing's just not in my blood."

"You're going to be very sorry for this, Mr. Mc-Cabe," she warned.

"I'll take my chances." Bates swung a towel over his shoulder and grinned. She looked good, he thought suddenly. Very good. The turquoise swimsuit hugged her curvacious figure and contrasted nicely with her soft creamy skin.

Rhetta walked toward the hotel's indoor pool with a challenging glint in her eye. That was one thing he could never resist, a challenge.

The pool was empty save for Rhetta, Bates and a middle-aged couple thoroughly involved with reading; she, the *New York Times Book Review* and he, a Louis L'Amour novel.

The water was an inviting green and looked as if it would be as soothing as a cool bath after a hot game of tennis. And as for Rhetta, being with Bates always made her feel hot.

She walked down the steps into the cool water without pausing. Bates dove in from the side and emerged beside her.

She nodded to him, smiled and swam the butterfly stroke over to the far end, showing that she was not a novice when it came to swimming.

Bates joined her there, water droplets clinging to his face. "Do we start from the side or do we do a racer's dive?"

"Let's do it like the pros—a racer's dive."

He nodded once and pulled himself out of the water. "You're on," he said, challenging her directly.

Rhetta climbed up the ladder at the side and walked to stand beside Bates at the edge of the pool. "Freestyle up and butterfly back. Loser has to cook dinner for the winner," Rhetta said calmly.

"Better yet, winner buys dinner for the loser." Bates stood and took a deep breath, expanding his chest. With the clean fluid lines of a swimmer or a long-distance runner, he was fully comfortable with his body and graceful because of it.

"You start the race." Rhetta bent her body and pointed her arms into the shape of an arrow.

"On your mark, get set, go!" he shouted, and paused momentarily to make sure she had gone into the water on time before springing nimbly off the side to land a full body length ahead of her.

Rhetta kicked hard to bring herself nearly even with him and to pull ahead. She was out of shape; one length of the pool and she was already winded. When they turned at the end of the pool he was still a full body length ahead of her, and Rhetta hadn't counted on the butterfly being his strong suit. Also, she'd thought he'd at least be somewhat out of shape after all the hours of hard work he'd been putting in.

He finished the second length and waited for her, hardly winded at all. Rhetta swam the remainder of the distance at a leisurely pace to catch her breath. Reaching the end of the pool, she turned over on her back to float and rest.

He swam up beside her and kissed her mouth. Startled, Rhetta grabbed his shoulder and looked at him.

He searched her face as if committing her features to memory and reluctantly said, "I've got to run." His gaze ran over her blurry curves beneath the surface of the water, and then he swam quickly to the side and pulled himself out. "I'll be back before dark," he called out.

As Rhetta watched him briskly toweling himself off, an inexplicable sense of fear claimed her.

She waved to him as he headed for his room, which was right next to hers and joined to hers by a luxurious suite. Climbing up the steps and out of the water, Rhetta lay down on her beach towel to dry.

Rhetta tried to block out her irrational fears, but they kept coming back again and again. Bates was meeting with the men and women who would decide their future. That's all she should concentrate on right now. The future of Bates's entire company rested with his new invention. If the computer supply company bought it, Bates's business was virtually home free. But if they didn't ...

After waiting a comfortable amount of time for Bates to leave for his meeting, Rhetta left the pool area for her room.

* * *

Stepping out of the shower onto the cotton towel rug, Rhetta felt refreshed and revitalized. She'd made up her mind. Tonight was the night.

She stood nude in front of the short mirror above the sink and sprinkled some powder onto her stomach. With one ear tuned to the television and one ear tuned to listen for the sound of the door, she slathered lotion on her just-shaved legs.

No artifice here, she thought, as she picked up the scanty lace bra and panties in a rich shade of coral and slipped into them. She'd made up her mind. Tonight was the night. Rhetta didn't meet her eyes in the mirror but bent over to brush her hair into a full, fluffy style that made her look far more glamorous than she had ever imagined she could.

She walked across the room and slipped into the black silk dress lying on the bed. She was in love with Bates McCabe, and she wanted him to make love to her for just one night. Then, if he left, at least she would have the memory to sustain her.

She went to the dresser again and applied a glossy pink shade of lipstick to her lips and then walked into the lounge that adjoined his room and sat down by the window to ease her jittery nerves. She stood up and pulled the curtains open so that she could see all the city lights come on. It was dusk.

Bates had promised he'd return before dark. No, he hadn't promised, but he had said that he'd be back. She sat down, crossed and recrossed her legs, liking the slithery feel her expensive stockings gave her legs. She turned off the television set and walked over to the window, sat down again and smoothed her dress.

A footstep sounded outside, barely discernible with the thick carpeting, and Rhetta tensed. She heard a key turn the lock over. Bates walked into the lounge, shut the door behind him and ran his fingers through his hair.

Rhetta stood up, silhouetted by the dying light from the window. "How did it go?" she asked nervously, rubbing the silk of her dress between her fingers.

Bates shrugged and laughed. "I'm almost afraid to say." He tossed his keys on the table and walked over to her.

"They didn't buy it?" Rhetta asked, fearing the worst.

"No, they bought it. In fact, they think it will go over big. Really big."

"Then why aren't you excited? Why aren't you jumping up and down for joy?"

"Because...because it's almost too good to be true. I kept telling myself that if this didn't go through, I could still make it...but I don't think I could have." He sat down and pulled her into his lap.

He didn't touch her, though. He just sat there, going over her features one by one with narrowed eyes. When his gaze rested on her lips, Rhetta swayed forward and watched as his lips took hers. Then she closed her eyes.

His kisses were sweet and tender, gentle. She was surprised. She had expected a burning desire for release after all he'd been through, an aggressive physical forcefulness.

He pulled away from her and stared into her eyes, and took a shaky breath. His eyes were a luminous blue, all consuming. Rhetta met his gaze with a steady stare of her own and reached up to unfasten her dress.

Bates stopped her fingers as they reached behind her back to release the catch. He turned her slowly around, running his hands across the silken material of her dress, and placed a slow kiss where the clasp fastened.

Rhetta released a long breath of air when he released the clasp and placed tiny kisses along her spine as he released each button. He slid the material off her shoulders, the dress landing in a small puddle at her feet.

Rhetta stepped out of her hose and, without turning around, laced her fingers through his and led him into her bedroom. At the side of the bed, she turned around to face him and reached up to loosen his tie, which she tossed to the side. She ran her long fingernails across the breadth of his shoulders and then opened his shirt, planting kisses, just as he had, at each point where she released a button. She pulled his shirt from his pants, then watched while he undid his cuff links, placing them on the dressing table with a tinkling sound.

Still standing, Bates leaned over her and brushed his lips across hers, tantalizing her with his nearness, and then kissed the hollow of her delicate collarbone. Rhetta felt a chill ripple like a slowly building tide along her skin, sensitizing her to the pleasant roughness of his beard.

She clutched at his waist, as if afraid she might melt with desire, and he trailed a finger down between the deep cleavage of her breasts. Rhetta moaned softly as he deftly released the catch at the front of her bra with no more than a flick of two fingers, and the bra opened to reveal the creamy fullness of her breasts.

Bates guided her down to sit on the bed. He knelt down in front of her and, with a feather-light touch, slid the bra straps off her shoulders, then stroked her breasts gently, without ever touching the tips. Rhetta's breath caught and held. She was afraid he would stop, afraid he wouldn't continue. She released her breath in one long sighing moan as his palms cupped her breasts, his thumbs pressing in, giving Rhetta the gratification she had desired.

She lay supine on the bed, warm and yielding, and Bates leaned over her. Sliding her silken panties down her hips and tossing them to the side, Bates stood before her, his eyes glazed and on fire with desire. He quickly stepped out of his slacks and shorts, and Rhetta held out her arms to him.

Never had she seen a man so beautiful, so perfect in every way. He seemed to pause, hesitate, and Rhetta's eyes widened. He closed his eyes and with a deep animal moan, covered her body from head to toe with his hard warmth.

Rhetta ran her fingers lightly over the muscles of his back, enjoying the sense of strength that she encountered. But if she had thought she would lead in their first act of lovemaking, she was wrong. Bates took over with a skill that should have alarmed her.

His strokes were feather light and then firmly rough against her smooth, silky skin. She moved against him, frustrated, and Bates smiled slowly. "Not yet," he whispered, and bent to take her lips again.

There was a sweetness to his lovemaking, a tenderness that Rhetta had not anticipated. It was as if he were cherishing each moment with her, easing her into enjoyment, so that when he at last took her, she floated away on a mindless ecstasy that had no beginning as she rode the crest of the wave again and again.

Rhetta squeezed her eyes shut, willing the tears not to fall, not to show him how much this meant to her. She wanted him forever and forever. Always and forever.

But he was the last person she'd ever tell.

Rhetta awakened first, feeling warm, and languid, totally alive and very feminine. She raised her head slightly from his chest and looked at his strong, uncompromising male features and wanted him more than ever.

She wanted to marry Bates and have a family. Rhetta swallowed her tears. It was so unfair to have waited all these years and to have gone through all the various stages of dating and infatuation, only to find out that the man of her dreams was "not the marrying kind." That was what everyone said about Bates. They'd said so from the very beginning. And he certainly hadn't ever mentioned anything about marriage to her. Or love either, for that matter.

Rhetta wanted to be filled with the deep shining light she saw in Sarah's eyes, in Nanny's eyes. The glow that came from being loved and loving in return. But that light would never shine from her eyes because Bates McCabe would never settle down. She'd known that from the start.

She needed to slow down, rein in her emotions and prepare herself for the day he would leave. Because now it wasn't the failure of his business that would drive him away, but the success.

Bates would get bored, want to expand. He had that driven kind of personality and would never put down roots. From the very beginning Rhetta had known it was inevitable. He'd said it at the first town meeting: "Tuckerville's plant will only be the beginning. I have plans to build and operate three more plants in the next five years." Those words had a haunting quality to them now. Rhetta closed her eyes tightly. He'd be leaving soon.

Bates stirred, and she looked up at him and watched his lids slowly open. He sat up and kissed the top of her head. With one hand stroking her body gently, Bates fumbled for the telephone by the bed.

He punched a button and lifted the receiver to his ear. "Send up the food and champagne I ordered. Now." He dropped the phone back on its hook and kissed Rhetta firmly before turning on the bedside lamp.

"They won't be here for hours," she said softly.

"Yes they will. Before I came up, I tipped the room-service waiter half a twenty and told him I'd give him the other half if he got our order up here within five minutes after I called."

"You tore a twenty-dollar bill in half?" Rhetta sat up in bed, pulling the sheet up with her.

"Yes, it works wonders." Bates stood up, nude, unselfconscious and comfortable, and put on his shorts and his slacks.

Pulling the sheet up close to her chin, Rhetta lay back in the bed and looked up at the ceiling, not as comfortable with his body as he was. Nor with hers, for that matter. Hoping he wouldn't notice her embarrassment and comment on it, she tried to appear casual, as if she had done this a million times.

There was a knock on the door. "Don't go away," he said, smiling at her. "I'll be back in a minute."

Rhetta waited until he'd gone and then made a dive for her underwear and a thick robe she'd brought with her. It wasn't that she regretted sleeping with the one and only man she had ever loved, but now she was having second thoughts about how she was supposed to act around him.

She *had* to start pulling back emotionally, or she would make a fool out of herself when it came time for him to leave. And if nothing else, she would have his respect when he left. Rhetta steeled herself for his entrance as she heard him paying the waiter and taking the tray from him.

"Hey, what did you get dressed for?" he asked, grinning, as he walked in, rolling a tray before him.

"I might catch cold," she said easily. "I'm starved. What did you order?"

"Boiled shrimp, fresh strawberries, cheese, crackers and, of course, champagne."

"Mmmm," she said as she picked up a strawberry from the plate and nibbled on it. "This looks good enough to eat," she mocked as she reached for a shrimp.

"So do you."

Rhetta's gaze skittered off. She didn't want to meet his eyes, fearing her emotions could be too easily read by him. "Have you called Nanny and Justus? You should probably do that pretty soon or else they'll get worried," she chattered. "I heard there was a good movie on at a theater not too far from here. Why don't we go see it tonight?"

"Well, I thought we might spend the rest of the evening right here. Together." His voice was as seductive as a violin, and Rhetta felt it pulling her gaze toward his eyes, but she resisted.

"Oh, we can do that anytime, but now that we're in Houston, why not take advantage of the bright lights?" She hopped off the bed as if she was full of energy and picked a shrimp off the bed of ice and dunked it in the red sauce.

"Rhetta?" Bates stood still beside the bed, champagne in hand, a puzzled light in his eyes. "What's wrong?" he asked quietly.

"Nothing." Rhetta went to the closet and selected a dress, keeping her back to him.

"Is it because of... Is it because we made love? Didn't you want to?"

"Of course I wanted to—I wouldn't have done it if I hadn't wanted to," she added quietly, turning her head to one side so that he could hear her.

"Didn't you enjoy it?" His voice was husky.

Rhetta batted her eyes to keep the tears back. How could she tell him it was the most beautiful thing that had ever happened to her? That being with him made her heart so full it nearly burst with love? That being without him made her feel so empty that she couldn't think of anything else? How could she tell a man like Bates that and keep her pride intact?

Rhetta swallowed and managed a rather shaky reply. "I'm... I'm not feeling very well, Bates. I think I just need to be alone." Without waiting for his answer, she walked swiftly into the bathroom and locked the door.

Chapter Eleven

"Hey, hey! Bates my boy!" Earl Miller exclaimed as Bates came down to the dinner table. "How's it going? I hear you're really making the computer industry sit up and take notice."

Bates sat down at his usual place at the table to wait for dinner to be served. "I'm trying, Earl, I'm trying," he said dryly to the twin.

"Yeah-boy! I always told Merle that if there was one man who could bring Tuckerville around, it was you. Didn't I, Merle?" he asked his shy twin brother.

Ignoring Earl's fair-weather comment, Bates watched as the other boarders shuffled in: Joey Heckenkemper, dutifully helping Nancy Henderson, Rhetta's assistant at the courthouse and at the library, into her chair; Douglas McFarland, the former minister, sitting down importantly at the head of the table; Ruth Lee, the old buck-toothed spinster who wore a look of seat-squirming secrecy whenever she was near Bates because she had seen him picking up Rhetta on their first date; and their newest boarder, Farley Hill, whom Rhetta said they really didn't have room for but that she'd been so insistent and persuasive about staying at the Tucker Boarding House that Rhetta had agreed to let her stay in the garage apartment out back.

Farley slid into the seat next to Bates, batting her nineteen-year-old eyes at him. "I sure am glad you were able to join us for dinner tonight," she said, and then hesitated, adding shyly, "Bates." She dimpled prettily and Bates sighed.

All he needed was a moon-eyed teenager drooling over him, he thought wryly. He nodded at her but cut short his meaningless remark as Rhetta whizzed into the dining room laden with a platter of sweet potatoes and pineapple ham. The white door swung once and she swished back through the door, this time letting the door swing twice before she waltzed efficiently back into the room with creamed peas.

She placed the vegetables on the table, never meeting Bates's eyes, and sat down to the left of Mr. McFarland and across from Bates. She nodded to the retired minister to begin the blessing and bowed her head.

The murmuring voices stilled as Reverend McFarland cleared his throat. "Our Heavenly Father, thank you for the bountiful feast you have laid before us and let us remember the hungry. Thank you for the long friendships we have developed here and let us remember the lonely and the oppressed. Thank you for the roof over our head and let us remember the homeless." He paused slightly and then added, "In Jesus Christ, our Lord and Savior's name we pray. Amen."

"Amen."

Rhetta took a deep breath and passed the rolls around the table. Mr. McFarland picked up the ham and served himself and then handed it to Bates.

Rhetta could feel his gaze resting on her. She tried to appear normal and cheerful. Friendly but aloof.

Ruth Lee, seated on the other side of Farley Hill, said, "Rhetta, did you hear Bates's company is talking about expanding their present facilities?"

"No, Ruth, I didn't," she said levelly. Rhetta looked casually over at Bates. "What are you thinking of doing?" she asked, her fork poised on the way to her mouth.

"Oh, just building a new wing." He shrugged his broad shoulders, as if to dismiss the importance of such a move, and leaned back in his chair.

"I think that's wonderful," Farley said, looking adoringly up at Bates.

Rhetta smothered her irritation at Farley and attacked her ham. "Yes, that's wonderful. How long will this take?" Rhetta speared a slice of pineapple and ham and carried it to her mouth. Bates watched her in seeming fascination.

"Uh, a couple of months." His gaze ran over her features and paused on her lips.

Was he searching for her reaction? A couple of months. Did that mean he wouldn't be leaving for a couple of months?

"Hey, Bates. I heard they're naming that big long street after you. How's that make you feel?" Earl Miller asked as he shoveled a bite of sweet potatoes into his mouth.

"Well, pretty good, Earl. Pretty good." Bates helped himself to some more creamed peas.

"An' I hear they're gonna name a street after you, too, Rhetta. It'll intersect Bates's street. Does that mean y'all are gettin' married 'fore too long?" He whooped with laughter and slapped his knee.

"Of course it doesn't," Farley said. "Bates told me he was a confirmed bachelor. Didn't you Bates?" Farley asked.

Rhetta kept her eyes focused on her plate.

"That's right, Farley, I did," he said complacently, searching Rhetta's face.

Rhetta stood up abruptly, scraping her chair noisily along the floor, and carried her plate into the kitchen. She placed the plate on the countertop and closed her eyes tightly.

It would have been so much easier if she had never made love with him. She had been such a fool to think that she could hold the memories and not want to hold on to him after she formed that final bond of attachment. Because in *her* eyes, they were one. They belonged together.

She brought the fruit and a platter of cookies into the dining room and laid them on the table. Not feeling hungry for any dessert, she picked up the remainder of the creamed peas and the empty platter of sweet potatoes and brought them into the kitchen.

Bates followed her with two more empty serving dishes. Rhetta could feel her heart pounding in her chest.

He stood to one side of her and said nothing.

She scraped the creamed peas into a plastic storage container, then slid it onto the middle shelf of the refrigerator.

"Hey, did I tell you that we may go to a second shift down at the plant next week if we pick up that third contract?" Bates placed the empty serving dishes on the counter.

"No, you didn't." Rhetta stepped over to the sink, turned on the hot water full blast and added a healthy amount of dishwashing liquid. Frothy white bubbles appeared immediately.

"Yeah, things are really running smoothly. I'm thinking of putting in Cal Grindstaff as the foreman. What do you think of him?" he asked solicitously.

"Cal Grindstaff has always been looked on in the community as a fine, steady man," Rhetta said evenly, putting the dirty plates into the suds.

Bates's lips thinned. Ever since their return from Houston, ever since *that night*, Rhetta had been standoffish. Pleasant, but removed. Aloof. Bates leaned against the counter and folded his arms across his chest. "I got a call from that man in Louisiana. He has a site he wants me to consider for opening up a new plant."

Although Rhetta's stomach jerked violently, she knew she didn't react visibly to the news that he was about to leave Tuckerville. She'd been waiting for this moment, expecting it. "That's nice. When do you leave?" Rhetta turned a plate over, rinsed it and then stacked it in the plate rack to the side.

"Oh, I'll probably head down there sometime next month."

She could feel his gaze boring into her. "Next month is two weeks away. Are you certain you'll be ready?"

"Come on, Rhetta," he said, grinning, "have you ever known me to pass up an opportunity, no matter what the lead time was?"

She forced a slight smile. "No, I guess not." Placing the last piece of silverware in the drain rack to dry, she wiped down the countertop. She heard the scraping of chairs as the boarders pulled them back, beginning the slow exodus from the dining room to the parlor.

Bates watched her in silence. He knew something was bothering her, but she wouldn't say what it was.

All the way back from Houston she'd been silent and morose. He was sure that she regretted sleeping with him. Women like her always regretted making love unless there was a wedding ring around their finger. She seemed to be retreating, rebuilding the wall that had separated them before. Sometimes he wondered if she even cared about him anymore.

She poured herself a cup of the coffee left over from dinner and glanced in the general direction of Bates. "Do you want a cup?"

"Yeah, that sounds good." He took the cup of coffee when she passed it to him then followed her through the dining room and out onto the front porch. She sat down in a rocker. Room enough for one, he noted dryly, and he chose to lean against the porch railing.

Rhetta could feel his eyes on her, as they had been ever since they'd returned from Houston. He was steady in his contemplation. Wondering what in the world was the matter with her. It wasn't easy for Rhetta to maintain her composure; he was spending more and more quiet moments with her.

"There's a new movie playing in Jasper." He placed his coffee cup on the porch railing. "Would you like to go see it?" he offered, anticipating her answer.

"No, thank you," she murmured politely. "I'm tired and have to get up early in the morning."

He heaved a heavy sigh, started to say something and then stopped. Rhetta didn't look up. A wave of relief that he had decided to drop it washed over her.

"Well, fine." Bates whirled around, walked down the porch steps and stood looking out at the night.

The door creaked open and Earl Miller poked his head out. "Rhetta? Bates? Want to play a game or two of Clue? Me an' Merle wanted to play some, but it isn't much fun with just two people playing," he explained hopefully.

"That sounds great," Rhetta said, grabbing at his suggestion like a lifeline. She expected Bates not to join in, but to her surprise, he did.

"Sure, I'll play." He stepped back up the porch steps, retrieved his coffee from the railing and followed behind Rhetta closely—too closely. She could feel the warmth of his breath on her hair.

Rhetta sat down at the dining room table across from Merle, the other twin, who smiled at her and pulled on his earlobe. "We figured you'd want to be Miss Scarlet," he said shyly, "'cause of your red hair."

"She gets to go first, doesn't she?" Rhetta asked, trying to ignore Bates's imposing figure blocking her light.

"Yes," Earl said, grunting slightly as he sat down. "I'll be Professor Plum and Merle will be Mrs. White. He always chooses Mrs. White."

"I'll be Colonel Mustard." Bates sat down right next to Rhetta and stretched his legs out beneath the table, rubbing against Rhetta's bare legs. She shifted a little, unnerved by the stalking gleam in his eye.

"You know I always thought that they liked each other," Merle said in a little-boy manner, tugging on his earlobe again.

"Who?" Rhetta asked, suspiciously.

"Colonel Mustard and Miss Scarlet."

"Yeah, you're probably right, Merle," Bates drawled, stretching his arm across Rhetta's chair and rubbing his callused hand up and down her arm. "Miss Scarlet has that man-eater look about her."

Rhetta ignored his comments and studiously rolled the dice, moving her red marker four spaces. "I hear they're going to try to start a senior citizens' home that'll be operated by the church."

Bates rolled and moved his marker.

"Yeah," Earl said, stretching. "I think it's a good idea, especially since you've been talking about turning this into a guest house." Merle and Earl both moved their markers the required number of spaces.

"I didn't know you were thinking of turning this into a guest house." Bates eyed her appraisingly.

"Right now it's just an idea. But it's something I've always wanted to do."

"Let's see." Bates looked down at the game board. "I suspect Miss Scarlet, in the lounge, with the revolver." Bates cocked an eyebrow in inquiry to Earl. "Earl, do you have any evidence?"

"Yes, sir, I believe I do." He surreptitiously showed Bates a card, which Bates recorded on his clue sheet.

Rhetta scowled. He *would* accuse *her*.

"Hey, Bates, where will you live if Rhetta turns this into a guest house?" Merle asked, then rolled the dice and suspected Mrs. Peacock. Rhetta showed him evidence and then took her turn.

"Oh, I don't know. I probably won't have to worry about that if she isn't going to do that anytime soon." He eyed Rhetta's closed expression.

That's because he won't be here. He'll be gone. Rhetta cleared her throat. "I suspect Mrs. White, in the conservatory, with the rope. Do you have any evidence, Bates?"

Bates silently showed her the evidence he had.

"Okay. Now for the final showdown. I *accuse* Miss Scarlet, in the billiard room, with the revolver."

"You're accusing already?" Rhetta asked, somewhat surprised by his early deduction. "You'll be out of the game if you've miscalculated," she warned.

"I know the rules of the game, Rhetta. I've been playing this since before you were born," he said dryly as Earl chuckled loudly. "I'm a gambler, remember?" Bates's brown hand reached across the table, brushing Rhetta's bare arm, and removed the three cards from the envelope. He stared at them momentarily before he tossed them on the game board.

Rhetta looked down at them. Miss Scarlet, the billiard room and the revolver. Doesn't he ever lose at anything? she thought with irritation.

"Well, that was short but sweet." Rhetta looked over at the three men. "Why don't you all play another game. I'm going to read the *Wall Street Journal*."

"How about it, Bates? Are you up for another round?" Earl asked, already preparing to play again.

"Sure," he agreed easily. "But since when did you start reading the *Wall Street Journal*, Rhetta?"

"As mayor, I feel it is my duty to keep up with the current trends in business so that I'll be able to make better decisions for Tuckerville." Rhetta scooted her chair out from the table and took the newspaper off the buffet before moving to spread the paper out flat on the other end of the table.

She heard them starting up the game and tried to ignore them. Him.

Why was it that she could be sitting twenty feet away from the man and be aware of his every move? She could tell when he was scratching his head, stretching or yawning. It was uncanny and terrible. She concentrated on reading. They continued playing, totally ignoring her.

Rhetta shifted her weight in the chair and turned the page. "You should think twice about building that new plant in Louisiana, Bates."

"Are you going to be building a new plant in Louisiana?" Earl asked, clearly surprised.

"Yes, I am." He turned and looked directly at Rhetta. "Why should I think twice about it?"

"It says here that the computer market is glutted and advises investors not to invest in any upstart companies. You just might have a whole lot more trouble in Louisiana. You won't have people who know you there, when the bank gets nervous about your loans."

"I'm not worried. They seem very eager to invest in my company," Bates stated confidently.

"Why don't you build onto the plant here in Tuckerville?"

"Because I won't be manufacturing the same materials. They'll be two separate operations."

"So you want to spread out over a five-state area? That seems ridiculous," she scoffed.

Bates's eyes narrowed, and Rhetta took her warning. "Well, I guess I'll see you all tomorrow," she said casually.

Bates's mouth thinned in exasperation. What in the world had gotten into her? She used to be so supportive.

After her departure, he excused himself from the game and went outside. Then he started walking. At first he didn't know where he was going. But he realized where he wanted to go as his footsteps took him in the general direction of his aunt's house.

He walked up the neat pathway, which was swept clean early every morning, and tapped lightly on the door. Nanny's blue eyes peered out the square window to the side of the entrance. The door creaked open slowly. "Land sakes!" she whispered. "What are you doing here? It's half past nine o'clock, and Justus is already asleep."

"Can I come in?" he asked brusquely.

Nanny backed away from the doorway, eyeing him thoughtfully and clutching her wrapper tightly around her. Without a word, she led him into the kitchen, poured two cups of coffee and sat down at the round kitchen table. She looked at him expectantly.

Bates looked around the tidy pale blue kitchen. The curtains were starched and the room smelled of lavender and Aunt Nanny's powder. The countertops were white, and all the appliances seemed shiny and clean. He looked back at Nanny's face and said bluntly, "It's Rhetta."

Nanny nodded. "I thought as much." She gave a grandmotherly grunt as she digested this information, clucked her tongue against her teeth and crossed her thin legs.

"I don't know what's gotten into her." Bates laid his strong muscular arms on the glossy oak tabletop, palms facing upward. "Ever since we got back from Houston, she's been different. Standoffish." He closed his hands into fists. "I mean I thought she'd be happy that I was finally making a success of my business."

"And she's not?"

"No," he stated emphatically. "Not at all. And tonight," he said, as if he still found it hard to believe, "she was reading all these gloomy forecasts regarding prospects for the computer industry from the *Wall Street Journal* and ridiculing my plans to build another plant in Louisiana."

Nanny nodded her head with a knowing smile on her face.

"It's almost like she's back to her original stand that my business is bad for Tuckerville." Ruffling his curly black hair with his fingers, he muttered under his breath in confusion and frustration.

"I don't think she really believes *that* bunch of hogwash anymore, but she does think your business is bad for Rhetta Tucker. Rhetta was Tuckerville before you came along—the queen bee." Nanny peered at him with round blue eyes and pursed her lips.

It made sense. She had a lot of pride in herself and in Tuckerville. But that still didn't explain how to get her back. Bates released a breath of frustration. "But, Aunt Nanny, I want Rhetta."

"Bates McCabe, I've known that since the first day you stepped up on the front porch of Tucker Boarding House and saw her," Nanny said drolly.

"There's not much that I ever did that you didn't notice, is there?" Bates grinned affectionately at his aunt and took a hefty sip of his coffee.

"Not much," Nanny said gruffly. "Now it seems to me that if you want to win on all counts, you need to start consulting Rhetta more about your decisions. Make her think she has a part in the building of your business, of Tuckerville. Rhetta is a good woman, Bates. She's like a daughter to me, and if you dare—" She held a warning finger up in the air.

"I know, I know." Bates put his hands up as if to ward her off. "You'll kill me," he said succinctly.

"I'll do more than that," she threatened. "I'll tie you to the oak tree on the courthouse lawn and take a switch to you."

Bates took a hurried sip of his coffee to keep from smiling at her threats. Same old Aunt Nanny. "Aunt Nanny, believe me, the last thing in the world I'd ever want to do is harm Rhetta. I just want to get back on course. I mean, things were going really well between us, and I don't want to throw all that away."

"All right, then do as I say. Rhetta forecasted doom for your business and she was wrong. Dead wrong. And now she feels like the whole town's laughing at her."

"She wasn't that far off. A couple of months ago she was more right than I was. I nearly did go bankrupt." He grimaced and ran his knuckles across the five-o'clock shadow on his chin.

"Well, every business has trouble getting started," Nanny defended. "Rhetta's just too proud to admit she was wrong about you. She's exactly like I was at her age. Proud and haughty."

Nanny nodded her head firmly, and Bates had to agree. Rhetta was proud. But he respected her all the more for it.

Rhetta left the library early the next afternoon and hurried over to her office at the courthouse. Rapidly she discarded her briefcase and purse on the green chair in the corner, snatched her coffee cup off her desk and rushed down the hall.

Just outside Justus's office she slowed her pace to a meandering stroll and sauntered into his office. "Got any coffee?" Rhetta perched herself nonchalantly on the corner of his desk and glanced down at the will he was reading. "When are you going to slow down and retire, Justus Burns?"

Justus filled her cup with the dregs of the coffee and unplugged the coffeepot. He sat down again in his chair and scooted up to his desk. "When they get another lawyer in town who can take care of folk's business properly. And in another month or so, I may be retiring. A new fellow's coming in from Beaumont. Tired of practicing in a big city and wants to do small-town work. He'll find plenty of it here." Justus chuckled, then leaned back in his leather chair and looked at Rhetta. "That's not what you came in here for, is it?"

Rhetta slid off his desk, walked over to one of his barrel-backed chairs and sat down. She raised her gaze to his and took a deep breath. "Before God, Justus, if you ever breathe a word of what I'm about to say to you, I swear I'll never—"

"Now, dad-burn-it, Rhetta!" He sat forward and slapped his hand on the desktop, the springs in his chair squeaking with his abrupt motion. "You know me better than that! How many years have we been tradin' secrets?"

"Since I was about four, but—"

"And how many times have I ever told a tale on you?"

"I don't know Justus, but—"

"Never!"

"But Justus, you weren't married to Nanny Fields before."

"Has this got somethin' to do with Nanny?"

"Is she Bates McCabe's aunt?" Rhetta shot back with equal candor.

"Oh, so that's the way it is, is it?" He leaned back in his chair again and chuckled, watching her eyeing him warily. "Well? Out with it, girl. The worst is over."

"All right." Rhetta cleared her throat. "It is about Bates." She cleared her throat again.

"You said that. Frog in your throat?"

She nodded and he passed a tissue box over to her. Rhetta pulled one out and twisted her fingers into the folds. "Well, I don't really know how to begin," she stammered. "It's very personal and upsetting." She looked up into his eyes for understanding. "Bates is leaving." Seeing his impassive reaction, she added, "You knew that, didn't you?"

"I didn't know it, but I'm not surprised by the news. Where's he off to this time? Alaska? Argentina?"

"No, Louisiana," she said, sniffing. "He's going to build another manufacturing plant down there. And he's leaving next month." Her eyes began watering, and she dabbed at them before any tears could start rolling down her cheeks.

"So?"

She sniffed again and looked at the clock on the wall, trying to keep her lips from trembling. "Well, I just thought, after all, I mean, we—we were kind of dating, and I just thought that he felt the same way I do."

"Are you in love with him, girl?" he barked.

Rhetta nodded her head. "Yes," she whispered. She felt so much better now that it was out in the open.

"Oh," he grunted. "Well, then what's the problem? You thought that Bates would feel the same way you do?"

Rhetta nodded, her eyes so full of tears that Justus was one big blur.

"Well, girl, he probably does. He probably loves you all right, but not in the same way you love him."

He looked over at her protectively. "Bates is a wanderer, Rhetta," he said gently. "Always has been. Always will be."

"I know that. I know that," she repeated. "But that doesn't mean I couldn't wander with him."

"Bah!" he barked. "You haven't got the pride of a goat!"

Looking down at her lap, she tried to pull herself together. "I love him, Justus," she stated with quiet dignity. She raised her calm blue eyes and looked at Justus, unblinking.

"I know you do, Rhetta. I loved Nanny Fields for forty years before she finally consented to marry me." He flapped his hands in the air like an old rooster. "And even then I nearly had to die to get her to the altar."

Rhetta laughed tearfully.

"Hell, if anyone knows what a bad case of unrequited love is, I do. It's in their blood, Rhetta. They're stubborn. And they've got pride, too." He jabbed his finger at her to make his point. "Stiff-necked Southern pride."

Rhetta sighed and looked down at the folds in her green-and-white checked skirt. "I know they've got pride, Justus. I want Bates to have pride. I want to marry him and—"

"And settle down with him and raise up a family."

Rhetta nodded her head.

"Well, ma'am, you've got the wrong man for that," he barked. "Bates McCabe will never do that. He's not the kind, Rhetta," Justus said earnestly. He stood up, walked around the side of his desk and sat beside her.

"I know that, Justus." Her eyes welled up with tears that spilled down her face. "It just hurts so bad," she cried. She fell into his arms, sobbing against his thin chest and cried hot, angry tears. She sobbed until she felt as if her heart would crack, until dry racking sobs shook her whole body.

"There, there, Rhetta. Don't cry over him. He's not worth it. He's not worth your tears," Justus murmured soothingly.

Rhetta felt as if she was five again, and Justus was consoling her over a lost marble or lost dog. Was she really destined to live out her life the way Justus had? Wait until Bates finally came around to loving her?

God couldn't be so cruel to her. She couldn't wait that long, knowing he was in some other town with some other woman in some bar or bed. Rhetta shut her eyes tightly and listened to Justus's voice droning on and on.

"...no man is worth that. And I'll tell you something else, Rhetta. If he didn't want me, I'd have enough pride not to want him, either. If there's one thing he should know about you, it's that you'll get along fine without him when he's gone. If he sees that, then maybe he'll change his tune," Justus offered hopefully.

Rhetta sniffed and her ears perked up at his words. "That's what I should do then," she said decisively. "Just start living my life as though Bates McCabe never existed. As if he wasn't even there."

"That's the spirit, girl," Justus said approvingly, slapping her on the back.

Rhetta smiled bravely but was all too aware that she was only playing a game. The only way she could ever get over Bates McCabe was to turn her love into hate.

"Look over here, you two!" Ruth Lee called out gaily in her falsetto voice, holding her camera poised so that it half hid her face. She snapped the shutter while Steven and Sarah smiled amid all the flashing bulbs and congratulations.

Fellowship Hall was packed, and Rhetta didn't recognize even half of the people she served punch to. But weddings were always like that. Relatives from every small town around converged on one spot to see off their second cousin twice removed or their uncle on their father's side.

Her gaze strayed for the umpteenth time to Bates's dark head. He was bent over, listening to something Farley was whispering in her childish voice. Rhetta angrily sloshed some punch into a cup and set it abruptly on the table for someone to pick up.

If I couldn't find anyone better to talk to, I'd just as soon hold up a wall, she thought, looking at Farley's childish figure, disguised by what surely was her prom dress from last year. "What? Oh, yes, she certainly does," Rhetta agreed, as Earl Miller passed by, commenting on Sarah's appearance.

"I guess we'll be seein' you in a wedding dress before long," Earl said loudly, and several people stopped to stare. "Or are you going to be the town spinster like Ruth Lee?" he said chuckling.

"Hardly," she said coldly, turning to fill more cups with punch. She wasn't *that* desperate, for pity's sake! Twenty-nine was *not* the end of the world. Lots of women got married after their thirtieth birthday these days. After all, she was a career woman. Rhetta squared her jaw and tried not to think about Bates.

There were other men in the world, even in Tuckerville. There were lots of bachelors in town. Pickings weren't so slim anymore, she thought with determined cheerfulness.

There were lots of things to be thankful for, she thought as she looked at the lively crowd in the room. It was a Saturday night, and for once she wasn't sitting at home with Ruth Lee and the twins playing Clue or Scrabble. She was at a wedding. It might not be *her* wedding, but still, it was a wedding. Something to do.

She drummed her fingers on the table in agitation.

"Is this serve yourself?" Faye Kern asked crabbily. Her hat was askew on her head and her attempts at pushing her orange hair away from her face had been unsuccessful. It still hung in straggles over her brow.

Rhetta pressed her lips together to keep from sniping back at her. It was bad enough being an old maid without being crabby like Faye and the other town spinsters. "No, Faye, let me pour some for you," she said politely.

"You'd sure never make it at my restaurant," Faye pointed out before moving on to the cake line.

"Then it's a good thing I don't have to," Rhetta muttered as she dished up some more punch.

"I think you can leave the punch line now, Rhetta." Bates took her hand and led her around the table. "I want to dance with you."

Rhetta was stunned. She didn't say a word, merely held her breath as her body came in contact with the hardness of his.

Rhetta was surprised he could dance, period, let alone be so fluid on his feet. His thumb caressed the inside of her palm as they moved around the room. He pulled her closer to him, and Rhetta shut her eyes. But it was too good. All she did was feel things when her eyes were shut.

She held herself rigidly erect and concentrated on the people spinning by. There was Farley pouting over in the corner. Sarah's and Steven's faces seemed to glow with happiness and love. She was at least glad about that.

Bates's hand moved down her dress, slowly caressing each tiny bone in her spine, reminding her of the night he... She shivered.

"Cold?"

"No," she said hurriedly, thinking he would squeeze her tighter if she said yes.

He chuckled softly then, as if he could divine her thoughts. Rubbing slow circles along her back, Bates leaned down to nibble on her ear.

"Stop it," she said, jerking her head back and glaring at him. "Someone will see."

"Good, then they'll know you belong to me," Bates said, grinning at her angry retort.

"How many other women belong to you, Bates?" she asked coldly, and pushed out of his arms. Pivoting sharply, she walked over to the punch bowl.

Bates stared after her in genuine amazement. Reaching up, he rubbed his fingers across his jaw in wonder. What was *that* supposed to mean?

A crowd gathered as Sarah and Steven prepared to leave. Nanny and the other town busybodies were running around, pulling all the single females into a group to try to catch the bridal bouquet.

Bates watched as Nanny practically dragged Rhetta out to the crowd of girls. Rhetta hung back, looking more forlorn than Bates had ever seen her before. His brain started turning ideas over and over, attempting to fathom the change in her.

Sarah eyed Rhetta, then turned around and, with her back to the crowd, tossed her bouquet in a high arc. The bouquet practically fell into Rhetta's unwilling hands.

"Oh, Rhetta, you lucky dog!"

"I wanted to catch that sooo bad!"

"Who caught it?"

"Rhetta, I'm so jealous!"

"Her?"

"Guess who's next!"

But all Rhetta could hear was the laughter that shook everyone from Nanny and Justus to Earl, who was nearly in tears, he was laughing so hard. She scanned the crowd for Bates's eyes, and he, too, was grinning broadly.

Without a word to anyone, Rhetta threw the bouquet to the ground and rushed from the room.

Bates's smile had frozen on his face when she'd turned to look at him. It had been clearly written on her features. But he honestly couldn't believe it. But then again, how could he doubt it after seeing her face? A woman that beautiful and desirable?

My God, he'd been a complete fool.

Chapter Twelve

Bates got up from the rocker and stretched lazily. He had tried to see Rhetta, but she'd been out all day. He walked forward a few paces and looked down the street.

Nodding to Minnie Bookerton who was sitting on her front porch with Sir Francis Drake, her dog, Bates yawned and searched the sidewalk for any sign of Rhetta.

He knew he could see her later at the town meeting, but he'd hoped for an earlier meeting since he had to leave by eight-thirty tonight in order to make his flight to Baton Rouge.

Well, hell, he thought, I might as well wait until I get back from Louisiana and do it up right. It'll only be a couple of weeks.

Chuckling softly to himself, he liked the idea better and better as he turned it over in his head. She'd be mad, of course, at least for a while, but she'd get over it.

He glanced at his watch. The meeting would start in half an hour. He'd go to Faye's for dinner and then head over to the courthouse.

The courthouse resounded with footsteps; the heavy clomping ones of boots, ginger ones, barely audible along the wide passageway, and dancing ones that skittered and skipped all the way down the hall to the meeting room.

Rhetta stood at the lectern, waiting for the townspeople to find seats while they called out greetings and exchanged gardening hints and recipes. She scanned the sea of new faces mixed with the old ones. There must be at least a hundred people here tonight, she thought in amazement.

There was something exciting about Tuckerville now, something new and brash that made Jasper and Pineland sit up and take notice of their sister township. *Things were happening in Tuckerville.*

People looked prosperous. Old Timber had finally gotten a set of dentures. Jonas Neal had bought a great big shiny white car to replace the battered truck he used to drive. The church had paved the parking lot on its east side. And old Abel McGregor was building an upstairs onto his house to make room for his second wife, and her three kids. He'd met her over in Louisiana at the county fair last fall.

Rhetta coughed, then announced loudly, "The meeting will now come to order. Will the secretary please read the minutes of the last meeting?" She looked pointedly at Nancy.

Nancy Henderson stood up, blushing a little as she saw the size of the crowd, and read the minutes from the previous meeting. Rhetta kept her eyes glued to Nancy's profile, forcing herself not to search the audience for Bates.

She had nearly died of sheer humiliation last night at the wedding. It had been a horrible nightmare. Everyone had been laughing at her because they all knew that she was in love with Bates and that he wouldn't marry her. And she had caught the bouquet! It was, she supposed, ironic. As they said in fables, she was an old maid. Never, ever, had she been so humiliated. And as far as she was concerned, it was all Bates McCabe's fault.

"Rhetta?" Nancy called to her.

"What?" Then realizing the other woman had finished reading the minutes, Rhetta stammered, "I'm sorry, Nancy. Thank you. Are there any additions or corrections to the minutes?" She scanned the crowd blindly for raised hands, purposely avoiding everyone's face. "All right then, a proposal has been made to use the extra money in the city treasury to build a park in the new neighborhood in the Eastwood section of town. We'll now hear discussion on this matter." She looked directly at Faye, who was sitting, as always, in the front row, and nodded. "Faye?"

Faye pushed herself up from the folding chair and stood, her stocky, well-muscled body reminding

Rhetta of some ancient, orange-haired warrior. "Hubert Simpkins bought a brand new house over there, and the toilet had hot water in it. If that's any indication of how they build things over there, you can just forget it." Faye sat down with a bump, the chair creaking loudly and her white legs sticking straight out in front of her.

"All right." Rhetta tended to ignore Faye's complaints. Rarely were they relevant to the topic; Faye just wanted to complain. Rhetta looked out at several of the raised hands. "Yes sir." Rhetta nodded to a tall fair-haired man in his midthirties.

He rose to his feet. "I'm new here in town, and I love what I see in Tuckerville." He smiled widely to let people know he was friendly and not a regular complainer like Faye. "It's a wonderful place to raise a family, but there is a serious shortage of playgrounds in the new neighborhoods that are being built. The only playground is on the school grounds, and I don't like my kids venturing so far afield. Is there any way we could start planning to have parks in these new neighborhoods before the contractors start building them?"

"Uhh," she looked at the crowd and tried to spot Justus. "Is Justus here tonight?"

"He had another meeting to attend tonight, but he said he might stop by later." Bates's commanding voice filled the room as he stood, and everyone else in the room seemed to disappear for Rhetta.

Rhetta's eyes glazed over in misery, and she wanted to run from the room. Her throat constricted and her heart felt as though it was going to pound right out of her chest. She refocused her gaze on the blond-haired man. "I'm afraid we'll have to table this discussion until Justus can let us know something further. He's our expert—on everything." She smiled tightly at the man and then looked down at the notes on the lectern. "Our next item of business is an announcement. Jim?" She looked at the banker as he stood and walked to the front of the room.

Jim Hopkins smiled briefly, showing the friendly split between his teeth that made everybody smile back at him, and then he cleared his throat. "I just wanted to praise Rhetta for the fine job she's done as mayor of Tuckerville."

Rhetta felt her jaw drop. She'd had no idea what his announcement was to be about.

"It's always a very taxing job to be mayor, and with all the new businesses that we have been enjoying the past couple of months, it's been a stressful job as well."

Light applause from the audience broke up his speech momentarily. Rhetta's spirits lifted.

"And the next announcement concerns Mr. McCabe. Before Bates decided to bring his company to Tuckerville, we were facing hard times. We couldn't get business into Tuckerville because we had so few people here, and we couldn't get people because we had so few businesses. We were going in a circle, and the circle was getting smaller and smaller. But Bates—" he nodded to Bates and everyone craned their necks to see him "—Bates took a chance on us, and we took a chance on him. Things have turned out pretty darned well for everyone. But it didn't always

look that way. This winter was tough on all of us. Bu'
because Bates hung in there and Rhetta was willing to
stick her neck out a little farther, his business pulled
through. Tonight, I'm doubly happy to announce that
Bates's invention hit the market two weeks ago, and
from all figures in so far it's a phenomenal success
The trade journals are praising his invention as the
greatest thing since sliced bread, and that's only the
beginning.''

Jim Hopkins smiled as excitement overtook the
crowd and Bates received slaps on the back, hearty
congratulations and heartfelt hugs from all the la
dies—including Farley, Rhetta noted dryly.

Jim raised his hand in an admonitory manner and
continued, ''I'll just finish up by saying that it's be
cause of people like Rhetta and Bates that Tuckerville
is thriving and growing. Let's all give them a big
Tuckerville round of applause!''

Thunderous clapping reverberated off the walls, and
Rhetta saw Bates advancing toward the front of the
room. She smiled and waved to the crowd and moved
to the lectern. Bates came up beside her and slipped his
arm casually around her waist.

The applause went on and on, and Rhetta kept
smiling and waving. She looked up at Bates then, just
for a moment, and her gaze was held by the warm af
fection she saw shining in the depths of his eyes. She
smiled back and he squeezed her waist with his hand
so that she fell against him slightly as the applause
quieted down.

Bates stepped forward, saying, ''I know it's impo
lite, but I'm going to speak first 'cause I've got a plane

to catch in a few minutes for Louisiana. So, Rhetta, if you'll forgive me, I just have a few things to say.''

It was all Rhetta could do to nod her head mutely. *Going away!* Already? She couldn't think about it now or she'd scream, or cry, or both. He'd be back, of course. He still had to pick up his clothes. But he wouldn't stay long.

No one must ever know how badly she felt. Especially not Bates. She dug her fingernails into her palms and concentrated on Bates's speech.

"It's been a tough road," Bates said, and then paused. Rhetta loved to hear his voice; it was deep and mellow and warm, like dark honey running over golden biscuits in the winter.

"As Jim mentioned previously, there *were* times when I'd all but given up hope." He grinned then as he caught sight of Nanny and Justus, who were just entering the room. "But I guess when you were raised by a woman as mean as my Aunt Nanny, you learn never to give up."

The crowd laughed, and Bates winked at Aunt Nanny, who shook her head. "And then there was Justus, always ready to cut a deal with me to help me out." He raised himself up to his full height and his face grew more serious. "And there was someone who, though you may not know it, helped me more than you can imagine. She was dead set against me at first, but once I had the approval of the town, I'll tell you, she was my biggest supporter. Rhetta Tucker exemplifies what Tuckerville is all about. She understands better than anyone else what makes a town work, what makes a town a community. There's only one reason that I've stayed in Tuckerville as long as I have and that is because of Rhetta. I have a great deal of personal respect and admiration for her capabilities as mayor of Tuckerville. So when you're thanking me for bringing prosperity back to Tuckerville, thank Rhetta Tucker for making it possible for me to succeed." He waved to the crowd and then hurried out the door, never even glancing back at Rhetta.

She was stunned, shaken. She looked out at all the expectant faces. "Well," she said weakly, and cleared her throat to put some strength into it. "He always manages to steal my thunder," she said, and the crowd chuckled with her as they remembered the town meeting of long ago. "I'd first like to express my sincere appreciation for your support, not only of me, but of Tuckerville. You all *are* Tuckerville. Tuckerville is Tuckerville because Faye Kern will *always* serve egg pie instead of quiche, because Sammy Newcomb will stop by your house most every summer with fresh catfish he just happened to have left over, because Louise Hopkins has taught every child and adult in Tuckerville how to read whether they wanted to learn or not, and because Nanny Fields is the only woman I know who is just ornery enough to make Justus wait forty years to marry her."

The crowd whooped with laughter at this last comment, and Nanny good-naturedly shook her finger at Rhetta. Rhetta opened her mouth to say more, but the words seemed to stick, and she knew she was about to really let loose a flood of tears.

"Thank you," she whispered. "This meeting is adjourned." Rhetta walked swiftly from the room and out into the Tuckerville night.

Rhetta felt tired and old. It seemed as though someone had wrung all the life from her body and left her limp. She stirred the gravy for the chicken-fried steaks with a mechanical weariness. Pulling the gravy off the burner, she dumped it into a serving dish. She clanged the dinner bell and began putting the serving dishes on the table.

"Rhetta, I believe you look a little peaked this evening," Ruth Lee commented, her voice dripping with concern.

Ever since Bates had left for Louisiana over a week ago, everyone had seemed to look at Rhetta with eyes full of pity, especially Ruth Lee. Ruth Lee now felt that they had something in common, as she had been left standing at the altar nearly forty years ago.

Rhetta slipped a curl of auburn hair behind her ear, and let the white door swing once on its hinges as she retrieved the pitcher of iced tea and placed it on the table. "I feel fine, Ruth Lee. I'm not tired and I feel just fine," she said a trifle thinly.

"I'm sure you do, lamb," Ruth said in a sugary voice as she sat down.

Rhetta's lips thinned as she too sat down, keeping a fingerhold on her composure as she waited for the rest of the boarders.

"Nancy, I do believe that being in love has made you prettier than ever," Mr. McFarland said with a beaming face as Joey Heckenkemper escorted Nancy Henderson into the dining room.

It was true, Rhetta thought. Nancy fairly glowed. Why oh why did life have to be so unfair? Rhetta batted her eyelids rapidly to keep the tears at bay.

Ruth Lee sat forward eagerly in her chair. "Have you two set a date yet?"

Nancy and Joey looked fondly at each other, a feverish light glowing in their eyes, but it was Nancy who answered for them. "Around the first of August."

"Oh, boy!" Ruth Lee clapped her hands together and her buck-toothed smile was wide with happiness.

But Rhetta had had enough. "Ruth Lee, would you mind presiding over the meal and serving dessert?" she asked in a trembling voice. "I believe I'm feeling a little ill." Without waiting for an answer, Rhetta rushed out the front door to the porch. She heard their voices trailing after her in a bevy of confusion and concern.

"Lamb, wait a minute! I know just how you feel."

"Oh, dear! How thoughtless of me!"

"It's the McCabe boy again. The strangest look comes over her face when . . ."

Rhetta shut the door and let the screen door slam extra hard to block out their voices. She squeezed her eyes tightly shut, but hot tears cascaded down her face nonetheless.

"Everyone is in love and happy except me," she whispered aloud to herself. With this new thought, Rhetta broke down in earnest, muffling her sobs in the hem of her apron.

Rhetta cried because she'd wanted to spend the next fifty years yelling at Bates on Monday nights for watching football with the boys and hollering at him on rainy Saturday afternoons for tracking mud across her clean kitchen floor. She'd wanted to make him hot chicken soup when he was sick and homemade peach cobbler when he wasn't. She'd wanted to have a little girl who had his black hair and blue eyes and a little boy who had his disarming smile and to take them for hayrides on top of Kern's Hill on cold fall weekends.

Rhetta had wanted to plant tender early morning kisses on Bates's eyelids before she went down to make the coffee and put her cold feet on him to wake him up when she brought the coffee back to him. But now the wedding picture on the mantel and the bronzed baby shoes she'd dreamed of were gone—and all because Bates McCabe wasn't the marrying kind.

Rhetta cried until the sun was a hazy coral-and-violet ball on the horizon. She sobbed quietly until the boarders had all gone into the parlor, where the air conditioner and the television set hummed together to soothe Rhetta's nerves.

She was spent. There were no more tears left in her. Her face felt dry and tight from the torrent of tears she had shed.

As usual, Rhetta had run out from the dining room without her shoes. She rubbed the soles of her feet across the glossy gray floorboards and sighed. The red geraniums nodded from their deep green window boxes as a cool evening breeze passed through. The white wicker rocker creaked companionably in the dusky stillness as Rhetta sat silently on the porch. A few stars had appeared and twinkled faintly against the dark blue sky. Sir Francis Drake walked by, dog tags jingling, heading home for one of Minnie Bookerton's wonderful dinners.

Rhetta smiled slightly to herself. Headlights flashed across the front porch as a shiny black car turned the corner and skidded to a halt across the street. Rhetta's blood froze. Good Lord in heaven, please don't let it be him. A man stepped from the car. His shoulders were momentarily silhouetted against the dusky night sky before he started forward.

Rhetta looked frantically around for someplace to hide. She couldn't bear to see him tonight, not tonight of all nights, not when her heart was so fragile. Perhaps he hadn't seen her when the car lights flashed over the porch. The wisteria partially shielded her from the street.

Stealthily Rhetta slipped from her rocker and ceased its creaking. Crouching low, she moved as silently as a mountain lion to the darkest section of the porch where the bridal wreath draped over the porch railing. Her heart was pounding in her chest as she heard Bates's footstep on the first step of the short flight of stairs to the porch. She held her breath.

Was it her imagination or had he paused slightly on the second step?

Heavy thuds sounded on the floorboards as he came across the porch. She heard the screen door creak open slowly. Rhetta struggled in the darkness to see him. She blinked rapidly.

His back was to her. He hadn't moved. Without turning around, he said in a soft voice, "Good evening, Rhetta."

Rhetta sprang up from her crouching position. "Hello, I didn't hear you come up. I was looking for a bobby pin I dropped."

"Mmmm." He turned to face her. The moon was a small sliver in the sky, so she could barely see him.

A heavy silence followed as Rhetta attempted to gain control over her nerves. *What a stupid thing to say! Looking for a bobby pin in the pitch dark.*

Bates laughed suddenly, a low, soft laugh that sent tiny shivers up Rhetta's bare arms. "I was hoping I might find you alone." There was an undercurrent to his voice that made Rhetta's heart beat faster and her breath quicken. She could see the glint of his eyes and the white gleam of his teeth in the night, and she clenched her hands into fists to keep from shaking.

She cleared her throat and walked nonchalantly to the wicker rocker. "Oh? And what did you want to talk to me about?" Rhetta was furious that her voice warbled like an old woman's.

Bates walked forward and took her hand. She knew it was clammy and cold. He crouched low beside her and laid her hand against his cheek. The bristles of his five-o'clock shadow were oddly pleasant against her skin. Rhetta shivered.

"Rhetta, do you like me?"

"I don't think that's a fair question," she said softly. Rhetta looked out into the night, anywhere but at him and then swallowed before she met his eyes, which were clearly visible at this close range.

"Perhaps not." He took her hand and placed it between his palms and held it there. "Did you think about me when I was gone?" he asked, his voice just above a whisper.

Rhetta's eyes filled with tears, and she nodded silently, not taking her eyes from his face.

Bates took her hand, so soft and white against the swarthiness of his own, and planted a small kiss in the center of her palm. "Why did you run after you'd caught the bouquet at Sarah and Steven's wedding?"

Rhetta stood up abruptly and averted her face. She couldn't take any more. Why was he putting her through this painful exercise?

Bates stood up with her but wouldn't release her hand.

"Let go," Rhetta whispered hoarsely.

"I can't, Rhetta. I have to know."

Rhetta swung her head around to face him, her auburn hair swinging out and then landing in soft curls at her shoulders. Her eyes shimmered with unshed tears. "Because I'm the old maid and I caught the bouquet." Rhetta dropped her head and let the tears spill down her cheeks. "I was ashamed."

Bates took her face in his hands and kissed her lips softly, gently. "I'll never understand how a woman as beautiful and desirable as you couldn't know that a man was so in love with her."

Rhetta's gaze flew to his face to search for confirmation of his words. The uncertainty still lay heavy on her heart. The same glow, the same light that she'd seen in Justus's and in Steven's and, tonight, in Joey's eyes shone back at her from the deep blue depths of Bates's eyes.

"I really do love you, Rhetta."

"Well, I think you know how much I love you."

"I want you to marry me, Rhetta, and never leave me. I want you to be by my side when the first brick is laid in Louisiana." Bates paused then and swallowed. "Could you leave Tuckerville, Rhetta? Could you, for me?"

"Oh, Bates," Rhetta said, and reached up to put her arms around his neck. "Yes, I'll even leave Tuckerville for you."

Bates pulled her arms from around his neck and took her by the shoulders, staring into her eyes intently. "It wouldn't have to be forever. We could still keep the boarding house, but we'll have to be moving around quite a bit for the next five years, until we get everything going."

"It doesn't matter just as long as I'm with you."

"You mean it?"

The porch light flicked on, and Rhetta and Bates, still embracing, looked toward the smiling faces of Ruth Lee, Earl and Merle, and Reverend McFarland, who were all peering through the window of the parlor.

Rhetta looked back up at Bates, smiling. "You betcha!"

Bates's lips descended to take Rhetta's parted ones.

An audible sigh from Ruth Lee filled the air.

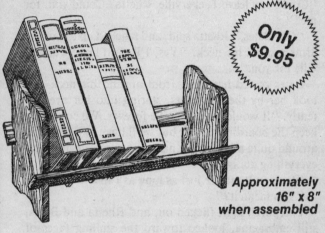

Silhouette Brings You:

Silhouette Christmas Stories

Four delightful, romantic stories celebrating the holiday season, written by four of your favorite Silhouette authors.

> **Nora Roberts**—*Home for Christmas*
> **Debbie Macomber**—*Let It Snow*
> **Tracy Sinclair**—*Under the Mistletoe*
> **Maura Seger**—*Starbright*

Each of these great authors has combined the wonder of falling in love with the magic of Christmas to bring you four unforgettable stories to touch your heart.

Indulge yourself during the holiday season... or give this book to a special friend for a heartwarming Christmas gift.

Available November 1986

XMAS-1